A NOTE ON THE AUTHOR

PATRICIA DUNCKER is the author of six novels: *Hallucinating Foucault* (winner of the Dillons First Fiction Award and the McKitterick Prize in 1996), *The Deadly Space Between*, *James Miranda Barry*, *Miss Webster and Chérif* (shortlisted for the Commonwealth Writers' Prize in 2007), *The Strange Case of the Composer and His Judge* (shortlisted for the CWA Gold Dagger award for Best Crime Novel of the Year in 2010) and *Sophie and the Sibyl* (shortlisted for the Green Carnation Prize in 2015). She has written one other work of short fiction, *Monsieur Shoushana's Lemon Trees* (shortlisted for the Macmillan Silver Pen Award in 1997) and a collection of essays, *Writing on the Wall*. Patricia Duncker is Professor of Contemporary Literature at the University of Manchester.

patriciaduncker.com

D0048204

BY THE SAME AUTHOR

Hallucinating Foucault
Monsieur Shoushana's Lemon Trees
James Miranda Barry
The Deadly Space Between
Miss Webster and Chérif
The Strange Case of the Composer and His Judge
Sophie and the Sibyl

Criticism
Sisters and Strangers
Writing on the Wall: Selected Essays

SEVEN TALES OF SEX AND DEATH

PATRICIA DUNCKER

BLOOMSBURY
LONDON · OXFORD · NEW YORK · NEW DELHI · SYDNEY

For S.J.D.

Bloomsbury Paperbacks
An imprint of Bloomsbury Publishing Plc

50 Bedford Square
London
WC1B 3DP
UK

1385 Broadway
New York
NY 10018
USA

www.bloomsbury.com

BLOOMSBURY and the Diana logo are trademarks of Bloomsbury Publishing Plc

First published in Great Britain by Picador in 2003

This paperback edition first published in 2016

© Patricia Duncker, 2003

Patricia Duncker has asserted her right under the Copyright,
Designs and Patents Act, 1988, to be identified as Author of this work.

Every reasonable effort has been made to trace copyright holders of material
reproduced in this book, but if any have been inadvertently overlooked the publishers
would be glad to hear from them.

This is a work of fiction. Names and characters are the product of the author's imagination
and any resemblance to actual persons, living or dead, is entirely coincidental.

All rights reserved. No part of this publication may be reproduced or
transmitted in any form or by any means, electronic or mechanical, including
photocopying, recording, or any information storage or retrieval system,
without prior permission in writing from the publishers.

No responsibility for loss caused to any individual or organization acting on
or refraining from action as a result of the material in this publication
can be accepted by Bloomsbury or the author.

British Library Cataloguing-in-Publication Data
A catalogue record for this book is available from the British Library.

ISBN: PB: 978–1–4088–7266–6
ePub: 978–1–4088–7267–3

2 4 6 8 10 9 7 5 3 1

Typeset by Newgen Knowledge Works (P) Ltd., Chennai, India
Printed and bound in Great Britain by CPI Group (UK) Ltd, Croydon CR0 4YY

To find out more about our authors and books visit www.bloomsbury.com.
Here you will find extracts, author interviews, details of forthcoming
events and the option to sign up for our newsletters.

CONTENTS

1

STALKER

I know that I am being watched. I think that women always do know when a man is watching them. Even if they aren't sure who he is. I can feel his eyes appraising my figure, following the swirl of my skirt. I feel the heat of his glance on my arched instep, delicate, visible beneath the leather thongs of my sandals. I take off my sandals to sunbathe, but even then a pale line reinscribes their shape upon my feet. He is fascinated by my feet. I hug my knees, gazing at my unpainted toes. They are sunburnt, charming, quite straight, a fine down of hair on the first joint of my big toes. All the hair on my body is a fine, pale blonde. I have always worn sensible, comfortable clothes, which reveal my body nevertheless. I am nearly forty, but my waist is as slender as it was when I was eighteen. I want everyone to see that. I have never been pregnant. And I have never wanted to be. My body still belongs to me.

Sometimes I wish that he would reveal himself. Today, as I walked back from the hotel pool across the uneven blue mosaic towards our rooms I could feel his gaze upon me. His desire warmed the nape of my neck. I felt the hairs rise slightly with the ferocity of his stare. The water was still on my back, my thighs. I turned, clutching my towel defensively across my breasts. I saw no one. But women always do know when a man is watching them. I know he was there.

I have begun to interrogate the face of each man at dinner. Is it you? Or you? Or you?

I do not always travel with my husband. Sometimes he is away for months over the summer and I hardly see him. This year he has earned a sabbatical and his latest dig is being sponsored by the government. So here he is on this island, early in the year, with his young team of underpaid archaeologists, all anxious to work with the famous professor. They scrape earnestly away at a crumbling wall or along the crudely bevelled edge of a barely visible trench. They stake out lines of string. They carry buckets of earth carefully around the site and sift through them for abandoned trinkets, fragments of pottery and bone. Over the central pit they have rigged up a corrugated iron shed, which creates a huge sharp square of shade. And there he sits, the great professor, the famous specialist who knows how to interpret layers of pebbles and sand, with his bifocals balanced among his freckles, peering into a flat slab of crumbling earth.

This sloping site is especially interesting. It has been inhabited for millennia. My husband knows how to read the layers of time embedded in the earth. In this place the foundations have been reworked and realigned by other hands, 5,000 years ago.

'Who lived here?' I ask, stroking the smooth, internal curve of a stone dish that has been found. My husband begins a little lecture on pre-ceramic cultures. This site is clearly Neolithic. For here are the Neolithic

2

walls, built in strange interlocking circles. I stand on the packed, dug earth and survey the pitted scene. My husband's colleague in Athens has sent back a number of uncalibrated Carbon 14 dates, which all range from 5800 BC to 5500 BC, the Aceramic Neolithic. I find their lives unimaginable. Who was the woman who touched this dish? Did she own it? Was it her mother's? Did she make it? Did she mix grain with her dark hands? I imagine her dark colouring, like Lindsay, with her dramatic black hair and big gestures, dominating the stage in the school play. My husband never knew Lindsay then, but he has seen her in the photograph, the official school photograph.

'What can they have hoped for? Did they have ambitions? Did they dream?'

I know that I am being whimsical. I look out, down the rocky white slopes to the coast. This view from the site is magnificent and appears in all the tourist brochures: huge sheer white cliffs and the tideless seas, thick blue water which near the shore becomes transparent, aquamarine, clear, bold colours from a child's paintbox. The earth is speckled with tiny white flowers, for it is still cool in the mornings, with thick, traceable dew, even so early in the year.

My husband finds me charming. He is smiling. He always smiles when I am self-indulgent, infantile; whenever I produce a little flurry of clichés. I confirm his right to patronize my sex.

'Oh, I expect that they were much like us. Except that they had to work harder to eat. This village may

3

seem a long way from the coast now. But the sea would have come further inland then. Look down into the valley. See the poplars? There's a riverside settlement there. Much smaller than this, probably because it was in a less defensible position. These people were almost certainly fishermen. Traders too, perhaps.'

Like all teachers, my husband is given to excessive explanation. He begins to tell me of the 1977 dig, sponsored by the Centre de Recherche Scientifique. They had no idea that the site was so extensive. My husband has sent urgent fax messages to all the relevant scholars. We expect the French to arrive any day. My husband is not an expert on the Neolithic period. He has stumbled across this ancient site by accident. My husband is an expert on the early Greeks. He is looking for the undiscovered marvels of the temple of Zeus.

The temple of Zeus. We have written records which describe the place. There is the poet's ecstatic cry upon seeing the distant line of the white cliffs.

> *Adrift in the wine-dark sea, our enemies far behind us,*
> *What joy consumes our hearts to view the temple of*
>   *Zeus*
> *Its noble pillars of Scythian marble, glittering high on the*
>   *sheer cliffs*
> *Of our native land . . .*

My husband says that the poets are often accurate geographically. And that the heroic deeds they record as myths are often histories, history as hyperbole, but history nevertheless. The battles took place, the heroes were slaughtered, seven garlanded bullocks were offered up to Zeus in thanks and praise. After all, my husband says, Christianity is based not on myth but history. And we have Pliny and Tacitus to prove it. But my husband has no time for religion. He regards that kind of history as wish-fulfilment. I see no difference between the resurrection of Christ and the transformations of Zeus. But I say nothing.

For he comes here, year after year, scratching the dry white and orange earth, revealing the agora, the baths, the granaries, the gymnasium with its fine smooth slabs, the fallen pillars in the temple of Apollo, the traces of forgotten offerings cast into the great pit within the holy precinct. It should be here, sited here, in close proximity to the temple complex, here stands the temple of Zeus. He initiates a new dig in a sector on the slopes above the cliffs and unfortunately uncovers the amphitheatre, which makes him famous. His name is now associated with this site and this island for ever. He publishes papers: 'The Amphitheatre at Hierokitia, a preliminary report', in the *Acts of the International Archaeological Society* (1986), and the big book, four years later, *Hierokitia: Early Greek Settlement in the Eastern Mediterranean,* Yale University Press, 1990, with 142 black and white illustrations, 6 maps and extensive appendices. As a result the site is included in the World Heritage List of UNESCO and is overrun with tourists. But my husband's desire is unfulfilled. His terrible, lifelong desire: to touch the noble pillars of Scythian marble, to stand where the robed priests stood, their sacrificial knives gleaming and purified, before the altar in the temple of Zeus.

I stretch out under the sheets with my legs apart and my damp sex tingling. He is not in the room. He is not standing outside the shutters, his eyes glittering in the slit cracks like a common voyeur. But I wish he were there. I don't want to see him clearly, but I long for his huge weight on my stomach, his face against my throat. Even with my eyes tight shut, or if he comes to me in darkness, for it is my desire that he should come to me, I shall feel his consuming glare drying the sweat between my breasts and the damp heat in the creased line at the top of my thighs. I squirm slightly against the sheets. I doze. I dream.

It is unusual for me to desire a man's touch with such intensity. When I was a schoolgirl I was in love with Lindsay, the most beautiful girl in my form. I adored the length of her arms, her swimmer's shoulders, flecked with drops as she surged into the 200 metres butterfly, and I sat cheering from the tiered benches by the school pool. You can't see it in the school photograph, which I have on top of my chest of drawers at home, but we are holding hands. We are smiling brightly at the school photographer, standing on chairs at the back, just behind our form teacher, in our blue cotton dresses with the wide dark sash, holding hands. Lindsay was head girl in the sixth. She won all the prizes: the English Composition prize, the Latin essay prize, the 400 metres freestyle, the Poetry Recitation Medal competing against candidates from three other high schools in the north Oxford area, and the Debating Society Award for Public Speaking. She never had any boyfriends and she was still a virgin at eighteen.

My romance with Lindsay went on for years. All those long revision sessions for our O levels, assessed by exams, when we were children, when we lay among the clover and orange hawkweed on the damp school meadows and tested each other on our quotes from *Julius Caesar*, when we were devotedly in love. And all those hours in the music room, supposedly practising our Grade Four performances, but sneaking every opportunity to kiss one another's fingers, ears, lips. She once left a little love bite on the crest of my left shoulder blade, under the line of my dress, where it would never be seen.

My love for Lindsay is all wrapped up with the smell of chips in newspapers, which we bought on the way home, and the huge swaying chestnuts and beech trees in the school grounds, held to the earth like marquees, tethered by daisies, where we walked in one another's arms. Everybody knew that we were best friends. Boys never asked us out because neither one would go anywhere without the other. Our parents said that our passion was a phase, which would pass. And so we remained inseparable. We hated family holidays, the depressions on the beach and the haunting of the Poste Restante in romantic expectation of the daily letter. I was the pretty one, short blonde hair cut to just below my ear and dark eyebrows, threatening to meet in the middle, which Lindsay wouldn't let me pluck. I pluck them now.

Lindsay was the clever one, games girl, prize girl, head girl, the effortless achiever with wide shoulders, long legs and black hair, the tall one with academic parents and three brothers, the one born with all the advantages. When she stood up to speak, everybody listened. And I was the girl she chose. I was her best friend.

But you know how it is. We were sent off to different universities, despite extensive machinations on the UCCA forms and lies told to parents. I went to Cambridge, read Archaeology and Anthropology and met Macmillan, the Junior Research Fellow, whom I eventually married. Lindsay went to Sussex and set herself up in a classy flat with wrought-iron balconies. She met another woman, with whom, so she told me, she had 'gone all the way'. How can you 'go all the way' with another woman? This was the most treacherous betrayal. Would I have minded so much if she had found another man? I shall never know. Lindsay never chose men. And so I sulked for an entire term and refused to return her cards, letters, flowers, calls.

Macmillan talked me round. He said you shouldn't drop your old friends when you get engaged. After all, marriage is only part of your life. The most important part perhaps, but not the only part. And so we all met up in a smart restaurant in Soho, which none of us could afford. I introduced her to Macmillan and the other woman didn't come. So it was Lindsay's turn to sulk.

But how beautiful she looked, still lean and tall, but fuller in the face, wearing a tight black top, the outline of her nipples visible inside her elastic sports bra when she took off her jacket. My thighs were glued together with wet hope all through the consumption of my carrot and coriander soup, topped with a thick swirl of cream. Macmillan delivered his first lecture on early Greek settlement in the Eastern Mediterranean, an elegant summary of current research and the latest finds. Lindsay was abstract and polite. I noticed that she wore little make-up and that her nails were cut short. I squeezed her fingers when we parted, promising to see one another very soon, but arranging no dates. She didn't return the knowing intimacy of my squeeze. That was when I knew that the affair between us was over.

I turn over onto my stomach. A faint sea breeze shakes the white curtains: fine, industrial lace, machine tooled, the curling swirls of a man pursuing a woman, satyr and nymph, his goat's legs, natty and grotesque, her backward glance egging him on. I close my eyes so tightly that they burn. How was it for you, Lindsay? All the world's eyes upon you, night after night. Did you like the world's eyes? Who was watching you? Who was planning with such intelligence, such vindictive precision, your very public death?

Lindsay de la Tour, her mother's maiden name, chosen in a feminist fit of patriarchal rejection, and then officially adopted as the professional *nom de guerre* for the stylish lesbian presenter of *Europe Wide,* ten thirty on weekday nights, the nation's heart-throb, the dream girl of the *Guardian* weekend features, winner of all the glittering prizes. It was chic to be a dyke the way she did it, with that drop-dead lipstick and those tight, tight tops.

She was every man's fantasy of the unobtainable ball-breaker, the short cropped butch with the long fingers and sportsman's thighs. She was the lovely lady who made politicians wriggle with discomfort, spoke French to the Euro-men, flirted with the lady mayor of Strasbourg while asking her a lot of embarrassing questions about budgets and corruption, the newsgirl who beat Paxman's viewing ratings, let no one off the hook.

'Didn't you once know that girl at school, darling? Isn't she the one we once met at the Soho restaurant?'

Yes. I knew her. We were best friends. Now she belongs to everyone. Now everyone can admire her wide swimmer's shoulders, her ability to corner her prey in a debate, her radical candour. She doesn't care if people talk. Yes, she's a gay icon, a lesbian figurehead carved on the prow of every politically sensitive project, her picture always on the cover of *Diva*. She's a success. She has all the necessary qualities. She is slim, handsome, self-assured, desirable to all men, all women, but hands off. She's untouchable. And she talks posh.

So who was watching her, following her, evading the guards, the porters, the locked doors?

Why ask who watched? Millions watched her every night. Why ask who? It could have been one of four million, or more.

But how it happened made the nation pause. I cut out all the reports and photocopied them carefully, because the newspapers eventually turn brown and dissolve. I carefully noted the police number we should ring if we had seen anything, knew anything, had any leads. I made up a little brown folder, an anonymous file of information. I became the detective, piecing all the elements together. But even I cannot know who he was, the man who watched her.

She lived alone in a West London maisonette. The press were discreet, the exact address was never revealed. She had a driver and there was a security guard permanently on duty in the building, which was under constant video surveillance. She never travelled on public transport. She wore dark glasses and scarves when she went shopping, like a Fifties film star. But she was so tall, so graceful, people often guessed. Are you, by any chance . . .? And she always smiled.

The first sign was a small piece in the *Sunday Times* in an article about a man arrested for stalking Princess Diana. He used to wait outside the gym where she worked out. He never made threats or left messages. He simply watched. He didn't seem to care if the police hassled or threatened him. He just stood, in the streets, in the crowds, at airports, behind rubber plants and giant ferns. He paid for his tickets, but never appeared to go home. He was an ordinary chap whose bedsit was coated in colour images of his adored Princess. She broke down in tears under his unblinking gaze and took out an injunction against him. But there it was, among the also-rans, all the other famous women who are stalked by men, with a dazzling colour picture.

Lindsay de la Tour, the glamorous lesbian presenter of the late-night politics programme, *Europe Wide,* has reported a persistent male presence haunting her street and following her movements. Police have been unable to identify or apprehend the man.

I cut out this tiny detail. It was my first clue.

But the news of her death a year later, splayed across every tabloid, on the front page of the quality broadsheets, the second item on the evening news, took me entirely by surprise.

Her body was absent. There were no pictures. Only distant shots of her front door, sealed off by yards of yellow tape, archival footage of her finest hours on *Europe Wide;* images of shocked colleagues, crushing their jealousy at her success and *schadenfreude* at her fate, pushing forward to tell the camera when they had last seen her and how happy she had looked. And there was the briefest of glimpses of the woman I had most desired to see, her lover, Helena Swann, chief executive of a major company, whose shoulder pads drooped with grief. I devoured the press. The police described the event as a 'brutal sexual murder'. But they would give no details, for fear of copycat murders. It had been like this with the Yorkshire Ripper. We heard whispers of a screwdriver, but not what he did with it. Not until the trial. We had to wait until it was all over to find out what should have frightened us. I videoed the news for weeks as the story gradually faded, and watched her vanished face, freezing for ever in blurred newsreel.

The police said that they were looking for a big man, a strong man, a violent, obsessive, perverted psychopath, the kind you might meet any day, who had left neither blood nor fingerprints on her body or on any object in her maisonette. Lindsay de la Tour was a well-known lesbian. This was almost certainly a factor in the case. They were looking for a man who was capable of breaking down the door with some tremendous engine. The reinforced steel bar supporting the frame had buckled and given way. Then came the other odd detail, the detail that stifled my hesitations, unleashed my characteristic decisiveness and drove me into action. *The police were quite certain that she knew who her killer was.*

All her colleagues and friends were being questioned. The police begged the press to respect her family's desire for a private funeral. However, the memorial service, a Christian occasion, public and sanctimonious, which she would have loathed, held at St Martin-in-the-Fields, overflowed into Trafalgar Square. Her murder was intensively discussed, with all the details breathlessly withheld. How vulnerable they are, these glossy stars of the small screen, always in the public eye, objects of fantasy, targets of desire. Her abandoned doorway was strewn with pink bouquets. She was lavishly and salaciously mourned.

I was alone in the house that summer. Macmillan was away, lecturing in California. After his amazing discovery of the lost amphitheatre at Hierokitia, he was headhunted for an Oxford Chair in Classical Archaeology and became as well known as Barry Cunliffe, a handsome chap who once dug up a villa at Fishbourne. Macmillan was then obliged to go on numerous lecture tours, armed with a carousel of slides and diagrams suitable for overhead projectors. He was offered grants, endowments, subsidies and visiting fellowships. He came home from the Archaeological Unit to consume his supper and be end-lessly praised. When he was away I fed my cats, watered the plants and dedicated myself to an intense regime of books and gardening. It was an exceedingly pleasant existence.

I have no children to occupy my time, and I have never wanted any. Children are neither tidy nor peaceful and I have always prized tidiness and peace. I hated the little part-time, underpaid jobs and extra-mural teaching, all the paraphernalia that kept the Oxford wives alive. I do not need money and I am never bored. Why should I work? So when Lindsay was murdered I had the leisure to speculate and to collect information. It was so easy to find out everything I wanted to know. You see, I had been Lindsay's best friend. I waited until she had been buried five days. Then I turned up in tears on her mother's doorstep.

They lived in Chipping Norton, just outside Oxford, up a leafy driveway with mossy white gates and a cro-quet pitch that accumulated puddles. Here was the house where I had played idle childhood games with Lindsay. Here was the tree with her swing, a huge rubber tyre now decrepit and shredded. Here was the sloping lawn her mother had begged us to mow in decorous even lines, mounted upon a huge green diesel chariot that sent forth a delicious jet of damp sawn-off green flecks into an inflated bag like a Hoover, billowing out behind us. Here was the next generation of untrampled marigolds and sweet peas. And here was her mother, shrivelled and old.

I stood sobbing on the doorstep. It was very effective.

Her mother drew me into the dark, rich spaces and clutched my hands.

'She was such a beautiful girl,' her mother whispered sadly.

And she had still been beautiful when they were summoned, as next of kin, to identify the body. They had seen her face; it was hers yet. And the police had spared them the photographs. But what had been done to her would become common knowledge at the inquest. Their solicitor would insist on reporting restrictions. Maniacs and murderers abroad in West London should not be actively encouraged. And the shame, the shame. Of course they had hoped that Lindsay would meet the right man, think again; it was natural enough at school, but after that, to persist! And look at you, my dear, so happily married to that nice professor. But this, but this. She had put herself at risk. Too late. Too late.

I dared not outstay the usual length of such visits.

My next move was clear. I took advantage of my husband's absence. I went straight to the police. They investigated my identity. They rang Lindsay's parents, who were pathetically grateful. Whatever she knows. Tell them. Tell them. The smallest thing may help. My speech was wonderfully prepared.

'You must not disclose my name. I am a married woman and my husband knows nothing about this. He doesn't know that I have come to see you. He must never know. You must assure me of your absolute discretion. I was one of Lindsay's lovers. I was her closest friend. I will tell you whatever I can that may help you to find the man who killed her.

'You say you are certain she knew her killer. I may be able to tell you what he would have been to her. But first you must tell me exactly how she was killed. I am not afraid to hear. However painful, however horrible the truth may be.

'She would have been killed in a bizarre, strange, theatrical way. And that would make sense. You see, when we were younger we used to play games. Sexual games. We understood so little about sex. We used to fantasize, make up stories, act them out. It was always only a game. But sometimes our small theatre of sex unleashed strange things. We were strangers to ourselves. Lindsay made up frightening tales. In her dreams she tamed monsters, hideous creatures that desired her. She was always Perseus to my Andromeda. I was helpless, the victim bound to the rubber tyre, or to the bent beech-tree branch in the garden. Lindsay played all the active roles. All I had to do was let fly piercing screams. She was the monster and the hero, the saviour and the aggressor. She became horrible, slavering, then valiant and chivalric. She menaced and tormented so that she could comfort and protect. It was all a game. We made masks, robes, shields and swords with real metal blades. But she never played the victim. That was not one of her roles.

'If the man who was watching her came at last into her presence undesired, then he had already overstepped the letter of his script.

'There was always a script. Lindsay always wrote the script.

'No man had ever touched her. She said that the first man would be the only one, the last one, her rapist, her killer, her unwritten partner, the man who watched.'

Ms de la Tour died from massive internal bleeding. She had been violently penetrated, both anally and in the vagina, by some kind of gigantic blunt instrument that ruptured her uterus and the wall of her colon. Her genitals and her anus had been savagely ripped open and torn. The lower part of her body was covered in sperm, clearly the product of at least half a dozen ejaculations. We are still awaiting the laboratory analysis, which has revealed certain anomalies. Inexplicably, her upper body was covered in garlands of flowers, which she had clearly been wearing when the attack took place. They were not placed upon the victim's body afterwards, like a perverted memorial, as was first supposed.

Then she died exactly as she had imagined that she would.

Who is the man?

She was waiting for him. He was watching her.

The police lean forwards and the tape whirls.

Her stalker?

'Women always know when a man is watching them. Even when they aren't sure who he is. Lindsay knew he was there. Maybe she liked to feel this man's eyes lingering on her buttocks and thighs. She was a performer, a presenter. Millions of men watched her every night. Why is it so exciting to feel that you are being watched?'

I have given the police something to think about, but no hard information. Lindsay's murder revealed to me something about my character that I had not known before: I am an astonishingly unforgiving woman. I think that this is one of my strongest qualities. For I have had my revenge.

I laid flowers on Lindsay's grave. I visited her parents. I began to do a little research on Lindsay's last lover, the beautiful managerial executive with the crisp linen suits, the suitably tear-stained face and the prominent wedding rings.

Then my husband returned from California and I had to put the project on ice, carefully secreted away in a locked drawer. My husband has all the middle-class virtues. He never pries into my affairs. I mentioned Lindsay's death. And he replied vaguely that it was a terrible thing. How terrible to know someone to whom this had happened. But we said no more about it. And the case, to my certain knowledge, was never resolved.

★

Here on this island, comfortable as a cat on warm flagstones, I think of Lindsay's murder, seven years ago, and feel the aesthetic satisfaction of symmetry. My husband returns, sweaty and pleased, at the end of the day. The French archaeologists have arrived and will be joining us for supper. Dress up, my darling. I want you to impress them. A pretty, charming wife of a certain age, well read, intelligent, with a slender waist, is an academic asset. I wear simple classic suits in pale colours, no jewellery and a single gold chain around my ankle, so fine it can scarcely be seen. That is my only concession. I descend the stairs. I sit down. I smile at the French, who rearrange themselves around me like courting lizards. And we order our aperitifs. I am the only woman present.

And then, suddenly, he is there. I feel the ferocity of his glare upon my naked shoulder blades and the frail nape of my neck. I dare not look round. His stare moves across my back, down to the neat curves of my arse, tucked into the light wicker frame of my chair. I am sitting naked, undressed by his consuming gaze. I sit a little straighter, bend gently towards the distinguished French professor on my right. I feel my stalker's eyes warm upon my back. His hands are covered in dark animal hair, like a werewolf. I murmur, nod to his attentiveness, terribly excited.

All the men around the table sense my excitement. They take it as a compliment to themselves. They watch my responses to everything they say. They entertain me, they please me, they seek out the erotic glitter in my half smile, my lowered lids, my charged sex.

My husband is delighted. Dinner is going swimmingly well, ushering in a new era of Anglo-French archaeological co-operation.

But, equally suddenly, I know when he has gone. I droop, like an exhausted butterfly at the end of summer, her wings tattered and frail. All the electric life fades from within me. I go out like the glow-worm at the break of day.

'Will you excuse me, gentlemen? I am rather tired. And I'm sure that you have serious matters to negotiate.' They all rise as I step carefully away, through the marble bar with the fountain of Venus covered in shells, into the overblown baroque of the old hotel. I pause at the desk to collect our key, peering at the blank green screen of the computer. Is he here? Or there? My clothes feel limp and creased, my back aches. But my stalker will have been satisfied by my performance. He will have appreciated the inward force with which I held myself, the curve of my neck, the arch of my instep, the fine line of my slender waist, braced to greet and receive his exacting desires.

There is something uncanny about the seagulls here. They are gigantic, with an unnaturally large wingspan, hooked yellow bills and colossal webbed feet. They are not tame, and yet they approach human beings with confident aggression. I lie sunbathing in the mornings for an hour by the pool. The gulls waddle close to my lounger, their heads jerking quickly towards me, then away, then back again. They rifle the dustbins, great beating wings thudding in the warm air. I see the cook, ineffective in his opposition, dashing out, armed with a broomstick and a living torrent of high-pitched Greek. The gulls are scavengers, pillaging the waste tips like gangsters, flying solo, shrieking warnings at one another. Yet they appear to act together, like organized squadrons of bombers, persistent heavy wings battering my balcony once my husband has gone, departing in the grey-blue cool of the early dawn. I am a little afraid of these birds.

★

It took me a year to find the woman who had been Lindsay's last lover – the woman she had been seeing just before she was killed – to make certain of her identity and to meditate upon my approach. All I had was the blurred photograph in the paper of her wet, twisted face. She was another woman, dressed in power and success. But the grief was real enough. One thing was clear: if I could find her, she would talk to me.

I have no close woman friends. I am a woman who prefers the company of men. Women bore me, with their cloying emotional confidences, their self-indulgent assumption that I will sympathize with their great griefs and endless pain. All the Oxford wives I meet have but three topics of conversation: their greying husbands, their appalling children and their inevitable disappointments, past and present. I will forever associate coffee cups with this long women's whinge of doom. Their second-rate college was the one their headmistress had especially recommended. She went there herself, but well before the war. The senior tutor thereof had always had it in for them, all of them, personally. And the old hag's motives can only have been jealousy and revenge upon them for being beautiful, clever and young. They were forced to abandon their research project, which would have made them famous, to become their husband's belittled assistant. They were always just too late or too old to apply for a grant/a scholarship/an award. They were bound to have won it, yes, certain, even given the competition, had they only filled in the application forms. But the resentments fizzle for ever. Their work was published under someone else's name, they were given an interview, but their age was held against them. The whining voice is always the same, and someone else is always to blame that they are second class, second choice, second rate, second best. Their view of the world is yellow, angry and embittered. From their comfortable, well-fitted pine kitchens and William Morris patterned sofas, they measure out the density of their disappointments. Envy is usually envisaged as pale green, but I see these yellow women in their kitchens, nurturing the fear of cancer in their drooping breasts and pluming up their frustrations, yellow and glittering.

I will not be thwarted. I will have what I want.

I discovered her e-mail address on the Internet: helena.swann@leaderproducts.net.uk and I sent her a very enigmatic message.

Return path: macmillan@ox.ac.uk
Delivery date:
Date:
From: macmillan@ox.ac.uk
To: helena.swann@leaderproducts.net.uk
Subject: Lindsay de la Tour

dear helena i am one of lindsay's lovers i must talk to you
for her sake use the return path asap sem.

For several days there was no reply. Then an urgent message in block capitals.

SEM NO IDEA WHO YOU ARE
IF   GENUINE   RING   020.7485.6823   X2718
   HELENA

I left the message gleaming, triumphant upon my husband's pale blue screen, and picked up the telephone. Her voice, so full of fear, was immediately reassured by my middle-class softness.

'Yes. At school. We were best friends.'

'I'm married. My husband knows.'

'I'm married too. It doesn't bother him.'

The relief in her voice clutters the line.

'The inquest. It was awful.'

'It's over a year ago now.'

'I know. It doesn't go away.'

'Did you love her very much?'

A deep, sharp breath.

'Didn't you? How couldn't you?'

Time to lie.

'I still do.'

She exhales.

'I do too.'

We pause, adding one another up.

'We must meet.'

'Next week?'

'Are you ever in London?'

'I'll come.'

'Can I ask you something?'

'Ask.'

'Are you afraid?'

'Afraid?'

'That he's still there.'

'He is still there.'

'But you don't think –?'

'What?'

'That it's personal. That we're next?'

'Yes. Sometimes.' Pause. 'Do you live with your husband?'

'Yes.'

'Does he know you're afraid?'

'No. I can't speak about it.'

Pause.

'We'll meet. We must meet.'

'Come then.'

'I will.'

'Sem?'

'Yes.'

'I'm being watched.'

She bursts out in an explosion of hysterical sobs.

But it is all well under control when we meet in her hushed offices, twelve floors up, with a view of the Houses of Parliament, crisp as a model cut out from the back of the Bran Flakes and Fruit and Fibre packets. We face one another and I see a great open sewer of terror in the back of her eyes. She is the chief executive of Leader

24

Products and so her days consist of meetings where fantastic sums are mooted and discussed, sales conferences, presentations and expensive meals. She spends her days making important decisions.

She met Lindsay at the gym. Please understand how it is. When your stress levels pass a certain limit of tolerance it's unwise to slow down. You need to work off the adrenalin somehow. I work out. On the weights. On the bike. I see her, sweatband sodden, cycling nowhere in a mechanical frenzy. Suddenly her chilly manner cracks. She is telling me the truth. I met her in the pool. She had the most wonderful wide swimmer's shoulders. She was strong as a man. I fell in love with her at once. When she took off her goggles I knew who she was.

The phone rings. Helena turns away, murmuring interrogatives. I flick through the prototype brochures on the glass table. She is considering new slogans and new designs.

* *LEADER – soft as a swan's feather*
* *A wide range of products*
* *Feminine hygiene and household necessities*
* *Try our new range of sanitary towels with added security wings for all-day comfort*
* *His & Hers – baby's brand new nappies – Xtra Strong – fully disposable – especially moulded and shaped for baby boys and baby girls*
* *The new move into lavatory paper: soft, white, fresh, environmentally friendly, fully recycled . . .*

Why do I find the idea of recycled lavatory paper so especially disgusting? That's all they appear to recycle. Perhaps the nappies and sanitary towels were beyond recycled redemption? Helena Swann terminates her call with a row of commands and returns to her executive settee. I smile brightly up into her perfect mask of under-stated paint.

'You seem to deal in nothing but excreta.'

And she has the decency to smile, suddenly anxious to know why I have sought her out, why I am here, sitting imperturbable amongst her cool green suites and glass tables, my feet sunk into her kilims from Kurdistan.

'How do you know you're being watched?'

She crumbles a little before me.

'I may be hysterical. Some days I'm certain. I've never seen him. I sense a shadow, just on the edge of my vision. It's so odd. I sense a big man. Huge. But I can't see him directly. It happens irregularly. Sometimes, in a restaurant, or on the tube, I feel someone's eyes upon me. Not just a casual glance, but a really intense stare. I look around. No one is there. Or I see no one. But the odd thing is that even when I can't see him, even when I'm looking, looking everywhere, I still feel that I'm being watched. How can I tell the police that I know someone is there but that I've never seen him?'

'Could it be someone you know?'

'Oh no. I'm sure of that. I work mostly with men. Some of them fancy me. One or two have tried it on. You get used to that. My husband is very trusting. There never was anybody else other than Lindsay. And think of my position. They wouldn't dare. Anyway, none of them is as big as this man.'

'How can you be so certain?'

She raises her hands helplessly.

'He just is. I know it. It's the size of the space he vacates.'

'The police say that Lindsay knew her attacker.'

Helena becomes white and silent before me. At the same moment I notice that her hair is not really blonde. It is dyed.

'I know.'

'Do you know how she died?'

'I was at the inquest. They said she was expecting him.'

'Why?'

'Oh, she was dressed, you know, she was dressed in a way that suggested she knew someone was coming. The table was laid for two. She had cooked an elaborate meal. She expected him.'

'Or someone else? Not her stalker? Not the intruder? Helena, the pictures of her front door were on television. The steel frame had buckled. The locks were fractured and split.'

'Then you don't know the truth. The door was broken down *from the inside*. She had let him in.'

We both stare at the diagram of a fresh white sanitary towel, soft as a swan's feather, bizarre upon the clear glass table.

Who is Helena? I am powerfully drawn to this woman with her doubleness, her power and fragility, her arrogance and insecurity, her certainty that she is being watched, her fatal name. I see us both, the widows, the bereaved, sitting silent in the mirror. I watch the differences. She is taller than I am, wonderfully, carefully put together. She is built for show, the front-of-house woman who deals with trouble and complaints. I admire her uncreased surfaces and velvet slits. I measure out the long curve of her neck, the smooth line of her jaw. Yes, she is younger than I. As she gets up to fetch me a cold glass of orange, I see the one element of her body that makes her female, tender, touchable, and which suggests raw flesh. I see the geometric rounded globes of her arse, swaying gently inside a smooth sheath of Yves St Laurent.

As she puts the glass into my hand I close my fingers around hers and look up.

'Don't be afraid,' I say.

All the muscles of her mouth tighten in disbelief.

★

The hotel receptionist has abandoned his post behind the computer in excitement. He rushes out onto the terrace, calling my name. Your husband is on the telephone. Come at once. Come at once. I take my time. Rearrange my silk sarong, which I tuck carefully into my bikini, and then stroll barefoot across the marble tiles. Macmillan is on the mobile. He has paid a fortune to make it work on the island so that he can ring me at all hours. I can hear the echo and crackle down the line.

'Darling, we've found something. At long last I think we've found something for definite. Come up and see. Come at once.'

He is a tiny child, calling Mummy on his new toy to tell her what he has dug up at the bottom of the garden. Macmillan is one of the reasons I have never desired children.

But I too have an uncanny presentiment that the search is over. I dress carefully, coat my nose in Factor 25 so that I look like an Australian fast bowler, and put on a hat. My nose turns puce and bumpy in the slightest sun. And if I am not careful it swells, lurid and pickled, so that I look a little like the Elephant Man. I am always very careful here, even this early in the year, before the sun cuts his teeth on the tourists.

I take the Land Rover and drive up the long white gravel trail to the site on the cliffs. The site office is abandoned. They are all massed around a flat square of pasture, usually covered in bobbing goats with bells around their necks and a mad shepherd who harangues them. I like this old man, hideous as Thersites, with his toothless mouth, unintelligible dialect and foul-smelling tattered clothes. He wanders up to me, demanding Coca-Cola. I give him money and he patters off, cackling. He is there now, leaning on his stick, his goats strewn over the slopes, resentful of the green wire fences, the extending barriers of the archaeological empire, stretching out like a flexible tentacle around the rocks and trees, financed by the Ministry of Culture and Historical Monuments. Here is a pair of cypress trees, one baggy and fat, the other rigid and penile, both stealthy, their shallow roots fingering the treasures beneath them.

Macmillan is in his element, standing over two of his diggers, who are now balanced on planks that spread their weight, bending carefully over the emerging fragility of a mosaic pavement. The white dirt is being removed with fine brushes. The tesserae are filthy, obscure, the patterns unreadable, each tiny square lifting its sightless colours to the sun once more after thousands of years.

Everyone is very excited. They watch each scraping movement in a breathless hush.

One of the Frenchmen who dined with us last night holds me steady on the loose pile of dug earth with a courteous, protective arm, and tells me that the pavement will be *magnifique*. Roman, of course, but *magnifique* all the same.

I peer down at the unrevealed mass of white earth. This means that we will be here for months, measuring, speculating, pondering this secret slope above the cliffs, digging an experimental trench, here, here and here again, taking dozens of photographs. We will be here when the first summer tourists come, spewed forth from the bellies of chartered planes, squeaking infants and bony teenagers, sixteen going on thirty-five, with dyed black hair and unearthly pallid faces, make-up which resembles bruising and ripped skirts revealing their buttocks. We will be here for the evening dances in the hotel dining room, with music from the Forties and Fifties that brings on indigestion. We will be here for the unspeakably embarrassing native dancing, which everyone applauds, puzzled. Here come the florid and elderly, courting heart attacks, dancing as if they were twenty-five years old, with nothing to lose. The hotel rustles up monsters: Elvis Presley lookalikes, magic acts, Greek men in white shirts balancing wine glasses on their heads and kissing fat, middle-aged women, who sit there shrieking, smirking, loving it. I will not stay at the hotel.

Macmillan stands radiant before me. Years of research and dreaming are at last turning to tesserae and columns beneath his feet.

'This is it, Sem. I know it. This is it.'

I embrace his enthusiasm, a little bored.

'I must book one of the beach cottages, dear. For the start of the season. The hotel pool will shortly become unbearable.'

Macmillan doesn't understand. He imagines that everyone will be flocking up the cliffs to view the site.

'Yes, yes. We'll have to think of something to satisfy the tourists.'

But not everyone bent on quick sex, hard drugs and strong sensations dreams of an archaeological solution. Nevertheless, over the weeks that follow a steady stream of fascinated visitors come to view the emerging pavement. The perimeter of the site is now staked out. Huge mounds of white earth are thickening on the waste tip. An army of wheelbarrows moves to and fro. The television cameras arrive and depart at regular intervals. Once more, Macmillan's wise face and imaginative Greek become well known on local television. From time to time he addresses the world, and we are obliged to set up a computer link with his colleagues in America so that they can keep pace with his discoveries.

There are three guided tours every day. My husband's students, glittering with victory and satisfaction, explain the excavation and its significance. Their explanations keep changing as the dig proceeds.

Welcome to Hierokitia and to the House of Zeus. We have been able to date this house precisely. It was built at the end of the second century AD. The mosaic before you is the first major discovery in this complex of buildings which we now believe extends towards the east, to the very edge of the cliffs. We are almost certain that these buildings, which we are at present excavating, were constructed on the site of much older structures. Some evidence for this has already been uncovered. Now that the bedding of the mosaic has been studied it is evident that it was laid using the methods most commonly employed in the ancient world. First, the ground is levelled and beaten hard. On this surface the builders laid the *statumen*. This is a conglomerate of rough stones and coarse mortar. On top of this they laid another layer, the *rudus,* which is made of crushed stone or gravel and pottery fragments, mixed with lime. We have found a good deal of rough, shattered pieces of pottery under the pavement, some of it painted. The last surface is the nucleus, a very fine plaster laid on top of the two previous layers. While this is still wet the tesserae are laid into it and flattened down. So it's a bit like fresco painting: the artist has to work quite rapidly on a wet surface. Very few of these figure mosaics are original designs. Whoever had ordered the mosaic would choose the figures he wished to have upon his floors. A mosaic workshop would copy the themes from design books. Sometimes the designer got it wrong and quite inappropriate figures would be incorporated into the chosen mythic scene. No, I don't know if the boss got his money back. Sometimes he mightn't notice.

Well, in this case we can see that the pavement was probably copied from an earlier pavement in a different building. The composition doesn't quite fit the available space. Look, the figure of the woman and the bird are quite central, but the tree with the perched owl is truncated, pushed against the hexagonal pattern around the rim. And here the basin with the willow – it looks a bit like a willow, doesn't it? but of course we can't be sure – is pushed to the left creating a slightly unbalanced space between the woman's left elbow and the fountain's edge. This kind of basin was not ornamental, but placed in the temple precincts for purification purposes. You had to wash thoroughly before you approached the god.

Look carefully at the tesserae. They are all cut from local stones, except for the highly coloured ones like the deep blue, which are made of glass. In this period there were massive workshops dealing with mosaic floors. So all the background filling, and even the geometric borders, were probably made and put in place by apprentices and ordinary builders. Only, the central figures, in this case the woman and the god in disguise, would have been finished by the master craftsman.

Now we know that these houses all followed a similar pattern: the *atrium* forms the centre of the building. The remains of a handsome colonnaded portico can be seen here and here. The solid curved blocks on the left mark the site of the base. Yes, they are very well preserved. We haven't found any of the columns intact yet, but the island was struck by a major earthquake in the fourth century and the house may have been abandoned after that. The colonnade extended on all four sides of the *atrium,* rather like a cloister. All the roofs sloped inwards towards the centre of the building so the rainwater could be collected in the *impluvium* – that's the little pond in the centre. This water was then carried underground in lead piping and stored in vast cisterns.

The main rooms of the house would be grouped around the *atrium*. So who knows what we'll find when we begin to dig to the north and east of the site. That's the excitement of archaeology. You never know what treasure will appear, hidden in earth. But yes, it's mostly old tyres. No, I've never been on a dig before where we've found something as unexpected and as beautiful as this. We dug up a medieval skeleton once, back in Wiltshire, and had to wait for the police to come and check that it wasn't really rather recent.

Follow me. But do be careful on those rough stones and try to keep inside the taped path. We dug an experimental trench here two weeks ago and some astonishing finds were uncovered.

Finds? Well, they're mostly objects. An amphora, that's one of these large vases, containing a mass of silver coins. They were Ptolemaic tetradrachms. Some dated back to 204 BC. More importantly, we discovered that this pavement was constructed on the foundations of a much earlier Roman house from the Flavian period. We could date the remains quite precisely. It was quite usual to build on the foundations of much older buildings. We still do, don't we? And that's often how things get preserved. The Romans used to recycle cut stone. I worked on a dig back in England where we discovered an entire Roman wall incorporated into a medieval barn. We had prisoners from the local gaol with us, who were doing a bit of digging, and it was one of them that noticed. No, I don't think he was a murderer. I think he was inside for fraud.

But the pit you can just see over there, beyond the gorse bushes, contains some of the most fascinating pieces of information about Hierokitia that we have yet discovered. It all fits together like a jigsaw. We'll have to wait for Professor Macmillan's research papers to get the full story; but I can tell you this: that part of the house was probably the site of the old kitchens. They wouldn't have elaborate pavements, just beaten earth floors, like some of the poorer houses on the island. So we dug through and came to the remains of earlier structures, no doubt part of the earlier houses. But that part of the site overlooking the sea is very special. We discovered a sanctuary, cut into the bedrock of the island. It was quite grand once, a big space cut back into the rock. The principal find, which was dug out by Professor Macmillan himself, was the ivory carving of a boy emerging from a slit, like a wound, as if he was being born. It looks like the ornamental handle of a knife. I think we would have made the connection even if the inscription around the base hadn't been perfectly clear.

IONYCOC

It looks like that. Can everyone see? The faint triangle is a D and the C shapes are capital S. Yes, the carving represents the birth of Dionysus. He was born out of Zeus's thigh. His mother was one of the temple virgins. You can read the story in Ovid. The maiden wished to see her royal lover not at night and in disguise, but as he really was. Zeus appeared to her as a thunderbolt and she was burned to pieces, but the child of their union was snatched from her womb and carried to term in the body of the god. Dionysus is a love child; he is the god of wine and ecstasy. It is quite possible that the makers of the pavement knew the sanctuary had once been here and created a pavement whose theme paid homage to the loves of the god. Taken together with the literary evidence in Homer, we believe we may well have found the ancient lost site of the temple of Zeus.

No, I'm afraid we can't go down into the pit. The sides aren't terribly safe. And anyway, there's not much to see if you don't know what you're looking for.

And so beneath this house and this beautiful pavement there may well be an extensive temple complex of significant dimensions and cultural importance, which will transform our understanding of early Greek settlement in this part of the Eastern Mediterranean.

Does anyone have any questions?

★

I arrange the move into the beach house. It is some distance from the town, built on the edge of a little cluster of apartments, attached to another hotel with a less glamorous approach through a grove of bananas. All the folded trees are brown and shrivelled; the golden hoards of bananas are encased in bright blue plastic sacks. Even here they have frost in winter. The cleaning maid is called Athena. She tells me that there were three days of frost this year, shortly after Christmas. We stare at the bananas, which now look like an optimistic folly so far north of the tropics. Athena opens the shutters leading onto the terrace. The steps are cut into the rocks, decorated with pebbles, and they fall away down to the sea. There is a rough stone beach, a tiny semi-circle without sand, and a mass of white rocks, flecked with long streaks of orange, dropping into the water, this eerie, transparent mass of lapping blue. There is something sinister about a tideless sea that stays clean. I prefer the hotel pool. I look down and decide that I do not like this clean, living water, which is unpolluted, ominous with the smell of fresh sacrifice.

We now have a telephone and a fax machine in the beach house. The computer is permanently alight with a large coloured slogan: PLEASE DO NOT SWITCH ME OFF, in English and in Greek, each word interrupted by Corinthian columns, and a motif of repeating black figure vases. A large map of the site is stuck across one wall of the sitting room. The students come here in the evenings, make thick, sweet coffee and leave a coating of white dust on the furniture. Macmillan sits, exhausted, indulgent and happy, amongst them. At night he lies peaceful beside me, snoring contentedly under a light summer duvet. Every day appears to confirm his initial hypothesis: that the rich man's house, built on the cliffs, covers the original site of the temple of Zeus. The shape of the sanctuary is now emerging. Yes, it was once a complex of buildings, constructed on a magnificent scale, a place whose grandeur and fame were reported abroad, a landmark 3,000 years ago in the unreachable past. Macmillan sleeps content, the fluttering of doves a peaceful rumour in his ears.

★

I am alone on the terrace in the morning sun, reading. The telephone rings.

'Yes?'

Silence.

'Hello?'

Silence.

'Who's there, please?'

Silence.

Silence, and again silence.

I slam down the phone, my fingers tingling. After weeks of neglect he is back. My stalker is at hand, watching, waiting. For this is how it always begins. Five years ago a woman began to receive his silent calls. She knew who it was. She rang the police, hysterical.

'But who is this man you say is stalking you?'

'He's there. There. Out there.'

'But madam, you yourself say you've never seen him.'

I was the only person who believed her.

Helena Swann lived in a large house in Islington, in an early nineteenth-century row with flat façades, dominated by barristers and politicians. There was a locked barrier at the end of the street with a large sign: NO ENTRY PRIVATE ROAD.

The wealthy climbed out of their air-conditioned BMWs to open the barrier and cruise through, nevertheless leaving their car alarms winking, the solitary red eyes alight in the half dark.

Helena Swann had a large London garden with an ornamental pond and an area dedicated to wild flowers. Here she cultivated her flag irises and marsh gladioli amidst her feverfew daisies, hairy St John's wort and water plantains. She walked in her wild garden, constructed with care, a carefully propagated mass of pink, yellow and white with a trim little cluster of lady's mantle and stinking hellebore. When she came home in the early summer, Helena Swann always changed into old clothes: jeans and an old checked shirt that had once belonged to her husband, and she walked out into her garden, unarmed, carrying no gardening equipment, to observe, caress and uproot with her bare hands, moving from place to place, apparently at random, bending to peer and meddle in the damp whiskers of cool green.

Helena Swann was particularly attentive to her pond. There were no goldfish, which eat everything, but there was an alternative mass of seething life: whirligig beetles, pond-skaters racing at random among the lilies, water-boatmen sculling purposefully along on their backs, then plunging out of sight, as if in obedience to an inaudible command of dive, dive, dive. And here is a mutant squad of tadpoles in the grip of inevitable metamorphosis. Helena Swann knelt at the damp edge to recuperate the shells of damselfly larvae hidden in the green. The original creature is hideous, a brown monster, a water beetle with foul antennae and grasping legs. They crawl, disgusting, down into the mud. But the thin fluorescent elegance of the damselfly, bursting into a resurrection of loveliness, abandons its monstrous beginnings and flies free. Helena Swann collects every abandoned carapace she finds and places them on a saucer in her kitchen, a grotesque collection of abandoned corpses.

Helena Swann walks in her garden in the cool of the day. She feels safe, comforted. She never saw her attacker.

★

The police were unable to reconstruct exactly what had happened. The woman had not screamed. She had been found by her husband hours later, half-naked and unconscious, sprawled among her cultivated foxgloves. There had been one great blow to the back of her neck and she had been brutally raped, several times, in her cunt and in her arse. No one had heard or seen anything. And there was one peculiar fact about the case, which puzzled the investigators. Her lower body was covered with duckweed and starwort, a long trail of slimy green maidenhair was coiled around her bare left foot and her remaining clothes were soaking wet. A strange trail of weed led to the edge. *Whoever her assailant was, he had apparently crawled out of the pond.*

The police came to interview me. I was already on file. They suspected that it was the same man who had killed Lindsay de la Tour eighteen months before. They knew that I had visited Lindsay's parents and that I had sought out Helena Swann in her floating offices high above the Thames. Let me tell you everything I know. I had said I would do anything to help. But now I tell them nothing, nothing.

Helena Swann survived the attack long enough to ring me from the hospital. She sounded perfectly lucid, uncannily clear, her voice urgent.

41

'Sem? Listen to me. There's something I didn't tell you. I couldn't tell you. I was too ashamed. About the night Lindsay was killed. I didn't tell the police either. I should have told the police. She wasn't waiting for him. But she was waiting for someone. We were breaking up. She had another lover. Her first name is Diana. I don't know her last name. But she works for the Chase Manhattan Bank in the city. Lindsay said she was a brilliant broker, buyer, whatever. She sells All Gold Securities. Something like that. She traded in some shares for me. Before I knew about her affair with Lindsay. They said they hadn't wanted to hurt me.'

There is a pause on the line.

'Yes. I'm still listening.'

'She was waiting for Diana. Not me. Nor the man who killed her.'

But my mind is already elsewhere. I am asking myself the obvious question. If she wasn't waiting for this man, why did she let him in? She could not have mistaken the huge form of her stalker for her woman lover. Unless she just opened the door without looking down the staircase and he walked straight in. But there was a security guard on the property. There were security lights which triggered the cameras covering every side of the house. The guard saw no one that night. Or so he says. The surveillance cameras revealed nothing, just so many kilometres of blank tape. The lights were never activated. How could so gigantic a man have passed by if no one saw him? Unless he was some kind of shape-shifter.

I say nothing to Helena Swann.

'Sem. The phone calls stopped. When the phone calls stopped I knew that he was coming, closer and closer.'

'Helena. Go back to bed and rest. Be calm. Get some rest.'

'Sem. Go to the police. Tell the police.'

'What can they do?'

There is a terrible silence. Then her voice comes again, fainter, fading away.

'Then warn Diana. Find her. Warn her.'

Sometime between twelve-thirty and three in the morning, Helena Swann was murdered in her private room at the Royal Free Hospital, Hampstead. Her neck had been snapped by some kind of blunt mechanical instrument, shaped like a clamp. There must have been an enormous struggle, for her duvet was ripped apart and the room was filled with clouds of feathers. No one saw or heard anything. Or so they say.

⋆

I sound extraordinary, even to myself. You don't know me. I knew Lindsay. I was her best friend at school. I believe you're in danger. I can't tell you what he looks like or who he is but I believe you're next.

Most women live with a certain amount of fear. But they usually fear the wrong people, the wrong places the wrong evolution of events. Most women will never meet the sex beast in the dark, no matter how assiduously they pace the deserted streets, picking their way through the abandoned newspapers. Most women will know their attacker well. He is their

43

neighbour, their uncle, their cousin, the priest they trusted, their father, their brother, their husband. Most women submit to sexual outrages far short of rape, and yet they rightly feel that they have been violated. Rape is the penetration of the vagina by the penis, without the consent of the woman, when the man knows that she does not consent, or does not care whether she consents or not (see Section 1, Sexual Offences Act, 1956). But have you ever been forced to lift your skirt before a gaggle of sneering boys? Have you ever had your knickers ripped with a penknife so that they could get a better look? Have you ever had the neck of a Coke bottle rammed up your arse while the man who has his knees on your back curses your stinking pussy? Well it wasn't rape, Your Honour. We were only having a bit of fun.

But another question bothers me. I am not, and never will be, the stalker's victim? Why? Why? Why had Helena Swann known this as surely as I do?

There is something impersonal and intensely intimate about this man's violence. His victims are the chosen ones. They are women in the public world. Women who earn men's wages, women who take decisions, women who take risks. But the stalker is not just teaching the over-reachers a lesson. He is establishing a connection with each woman first. He waits until he is acknowledged. And then he steps, invisible, over the threshold.

I sit watching late night television while Macmillan is on the phone to America. I observe that the serial killer has become something of a Hollywood hero. I peer at the speckled screen. She has locked all the windows, all the doors. She is eight floors up. But here he comes riding the lift shaft or scaling the sheer metallic surfaces with miraculous, magnetic, grappling irons. Technology smiles down upon the serial killer and unveils all her secrets with an open hand. Scream, my darling. Scream all you like. No one will hear you scream.

I decide that I will ring this unknown woman. I am the only one who has followed the case and understood all the evidence. I take the precaution of using a London call box.

Oddly enough, she is harder to touch than Helena Swann. I run into security mechanisms, blocking my enquiries:

Who's calling, please?

Please state the nature of your business.

May I ask the reason for your call?

I'm afraid she's not available, may I help you?

Hold the line please, I'll transfer you to personnel.

Pardon me, but are you a member of her family?

I cannot proceed without explanations. So I pose as a client with something to sell. And the doors open, the telephone rings and she answers, giving her name first, so briskly that I am taken aback.

'Diana Harrison. All Gold Securities. How can I help you?'

She is American. I am surprised. I did not expect an American. Behind her, like the backdrop sound on a film, I hear telephones incessantly ringing, a great roar of noise, voices unintelligible, talking rapidly.

'Hello? Hello?' Impatient.

'I knew Lindsay.' I simply make the statement. My voice is sharp and firm.

'Who is this?'

'Have you been receiving silent calls?'

'Listen, sweetheart. I don't know who the hell you are, but if this is a joke, I'll have this call traced and you prosecuted for harassment.'

'No joke. I was Lindsay's best friend. I was the last person to speak to Helena Swann. Please listen to me.'

'OK. Just a minute.'

A door thuds shut somewhere. The noise is cut suddenly in half. I hear a man's voice saying, 'I want everyone at their desks by 3.30 a.m. on Budget Day. I mean it.' The man's voice is suddenly conversational. 'Well, if the Chancellor abolishes the clawback on Advance Corporation Tax completely, British share prices should fall by ten per cent.'

'Have you been receiving silent calls?'

'Honey, if you've got nothing better to say then hang up. I'm busy.'

'Look. I beg you. If you get silent calls then ring 1471 and if the caller's number is withheld, then ring me. My name is Sem – 01865 722865. Did you get that?'

Mechanically, she repeats my number, but now doubt fractures her aggression.

'Yeah. OK.'

Behind her, the man's voice continues.

'Yeah. I know him. He's the city planner who invented the ring of steel, which is supposed to keep the IRA out and stop them killing us all. Well, he's offered to fish some newt tadpoles out of his pond for me. He's a really nice guy.'

She slams down the phone. I imagine the rest.

★

1–4–7–1

YOU-WERE-CALLED-TODAY-AT-TEN-FORTY-THREE-HOURS. THE-CALLER-WITHHELD-THEIR-NUMBER. PLEASE-HANG-UP.

'Geoff! Trace that call. I don't care how long it takes. Find out who is ringing me up.'

But she never rings me. The police do. She was found dead at twelve o'clock on the following morning by the woman who came to clean her flat. She lay by the telephone, naked, rigid and white, with her blank eyes open and staring, as if she were an abandoned classical statue. She had died of asphyxiation. The killer was perverted beyond comprehension. They found traces of semen in her vagina and in her mouth. And both her cunt and her gullet had been stuffed with priceless gold coins. The extracted gold was now being identified, dated, valued. The staff at the British Museum coin department touch this fantastic hoard with white latex fingers, amazed, wondering. The woman had been well paid with rich pickings.

There was one telephone number scrawled on the writing pad. Mine.

The police came to Oxford to visit me.

'We can find a very clear sequence of events and circumstances linking these three cases, Mrs Macmillan. And all the links we have bring us back to you. Do you have any explanation for this?'

But I have no idea how she knew my number. I have never heard of this woman. I know nothing, nothing. How can you ask me to explain? I am still terrified by the deaths of Lindsay de la Tour and Helena Swann. How do you know I'm not next? Oh, oh, it could be my turn next. I burst into tears.

Macmillan defends me magnificently and sees the police off the premises. I slip away to bed, and lie there, thinking.

*

Women's lives are the dark continent, not our sexual selves. You can peer at our bodies, legs splayed open, whenever you like. Our bodies present a deceptively simple script. But our desires, so often unuttered, are fluid, protean, inconstant. We cannot be measured; we cannot be assessed. Our inner lives are the hidden spaces. Sometimes all within is a murky coiling void, a black carnival of inchoate shapes and values. But sometimes there is a clear line of purpose, sharp and gleaming like a railway, an invisible singing, jutting out into infinity. No one knows what shapes our inner lives. That is our own business.

Look at the woman who gave birth to you. Look at the woman with whom you live. Does she sit sucking Prozac, nibbling chocolate, eyes fixed upon the television? Is she out of the door by six forty-five, well on the way to glory, leaving the washing machine set to full throttle, something for tonight fished out of the freezer and resting in the fridge? Is she waving you off with a fingertips kiss, still warm from the bed, hastily wrapped in her dressing gown? Do you know what she is going to do for the rest of the day? Did she tell you? And do you believe her? Was she still asleep when you left? Does she love her children more than you? Are you one of her children? Has she walked through miles of dust to find you? Is she still squatting in the back yard, reading? Is she minding the shop? Was she gone, one Friday night, with no excuses or advance explanations? Without leaving a note? Did she take all the money in the joint account? All that was left in the kitchen drawer and all her grand-mother's cutlery? Did she send you the divorce papers by e-mail? Do you still love her? Do you understand why?

Women never tell the truth. They are too canny and too firmly bent on survival. Do you hear her saying, Oh yes, I love my husband? I'm very happily married. Oh, yes, I like my job. I'd do more hours if I could. My children are my greatest joy. Oh yes, I'm very lucky. I love my husband and my children. Yes, yes, yes. Or does she confront you with a lengthy catalogue of self-hatred and doomed fortunes? I do not love my own sex. But let me praise a woman's cunning. She is a master of negotiation and betrayal. She says her piece and withdraws. Here is defensible space. And I will ward off all comers, with my giant structures of deceit.

I contemplate adultery with hard, steady eyes. I have never been unfaithful to my husband because I am not particularly interested in men. No man has ever given me his full attention. What they like to do is contemplate the effect they are having upon me, as I sit, radiant and gleaming before them, listening to their conversation. They fill up their chairs, very pleased with themselves.

But now someone is giving me his full attention. Attention is a kind of passion. I am being watched.

I know that I am being watched. I think that women always do know when a man is watching them. Even if they aren't sure who he is. He is fascinated by my feet and wrists. His desire warms the nape of my neck. I feel the soft hair rise slightly under the ferocity of his gaze.

*

I visit the site in the late afternoons, when the stones are still hot beneath my feet. The site is low to the eye. From a distance, there is nothing to see. The priceless ruins of the lost city lie abandoned in little piles. Only two columns still stand, erect on the far side of the marketplace. Here we study the infinite mystery of foundations. I pad softly through the white dust. The last two tourist cars, their pink plates thick with dirt, pull away from the car park. The sun is no longer vertical over the perspiring archaeologists, who squat like white dwarves along the crossed lines of their trenches, or sweat it out half naked under their green tarpaulins, their mouths pink and obscene, washed clean by fresh water.

Here I stand on the brink of the sanctuary. The emerging shape in the white rock is a crude, uneven square. This is the house of the god. I duck past the huge

succulents, great spiky lobes of conglomerate cacti, dripping white juice from their accidental slits. He was here,
and here and here.

There is nothing to see, just the white earth, peeled
back.

I avoid my husband and creep away.

★

The air does not cool as the evening advances. There is
water in my mouth as I gulp the damp heat, salt in the
trickle of sweat between my breasts. Far out over the sea,
towards the south-west, the sky blackens. I am overcome
with nausea in the shower and retch violently into the
basin. A yellow spiral of sick forms around the plughole.
I retreat to the bed and lie down. The first wind stirs the
white curtains.

Why am I being treated differently? Why have you
waited for me to give you a sign? You aren't afraid of him.
You've come back. You've chosen him. You sought him
out. Tracked him down. You forced him to notice you.
You looked up.

I feel his presence now, achingly close, hot between
my thighs. It is my desire that he should come to me. I
lie with my legs apart, stroking my sex. I pull the hood
back from my pink mound and thrust my fingers inside
myself. I want him to come. I am quite unafraid. I get up,
dim the lights, unlock the doors.

Then I hear a voice calling from the terrace.

I rush out, half clothed, and see a strange, tall boy
standing at the bottom of the steps. He is Greek, barely

sixteen. A giant motorbike leans behind him, balanced on a slender silver peg. His handsome, blank face scarcely registers my presence. His hair is an unusual reddish blonde. He stands, arrogant and uncaring, in the leaden, luminous air, grotesquely overdressed in black leather. His English is barely intelligible.

'I've got a message for you from the boss. He says he wants to see you. Get ready. I'll come back.'

When he turns around I see the shape of a chalice, etched in gold, glittering between his shoulders. He mounts the bike, which swells into life, and is gone.

Macmillan spends the evening in a panic-stricken rush of activity as the stormy light thickens. The team are stretching tarpaulins over the gouged earth, hastily hammering tent pegs into the unyielding rocky soil, weighing down plastic with stones, packing up the drawings and tools, setting out the buckets in a fire-man's row to catch the coming rain. The wind is rising, rising. And we hear the first mutters of thunder, far away in the hills.

But suddenly it is upon us, all around us, with the first lurid bolt of electric fire revealing the fabulous pavement of the half-naked woman and the swan plucking at her robes, in a white, illuminated flash. The makeshift shelters quiver in the gusts and the roofs buckle beneath the giant breath of hot wind.

Then the rain begins.

The blue plastic sacks shielding the bananas bulge and sag beneath the weight of grey, driving rain. The night floods in.

I stand on the steps in a white silk dress, which reveals my breasts and blows against my thighs. The sea shifts beneath me, evil in its caress. I look out. And there, coming towards me through the banana plantations, out of the boiling dark, is the single silver disc of light from a black motorbike.

2

SOPHIA WALTERS SHAW

My name is Sophia. But there are three of us. There have always been three of us, and the other two are here with me now. We go everywhere together. The taller of the other two has sandy hair and freckles. He looks pigeon-chested, unconvincing, but in fact he is surprisingly agile and very strong. His name is Walters. The third one of us is the most dangerous. He is the quiet one, the dark one, the one with the shaved head. A delicate spiky down covers his skull as it grows out. Whenever we construct one of our operations he shaves his head. It is a formal ritual, a preparation. It is as if he needs to alter his appearance irrevocably before he is able to act. He becomes a slightly different person. His name is Shaw. He has no other name. I think that we are all slightly different when we are working, but he takes the trouble to look different. Walters and I are never disguised. We appear to be who we always are. He is unassuming, but authoritative. I am the woman who is very well dressed. I began to dress up years ago. I never take risks.

I think of us, not as three single people, but as one. We are intimately connected. It is as if my identity is hyphenated, like the modern woman who, when she marries, settles for a halfway house, keeping her own name, but adding those of her husbands: Sophia Walters Shaw. I cannot imagine being separated from the others. It is as if there have always been three of us. But that is not so.

We first met through the agency. I was something of a wild card then. I was twenty-one. I had dropped out of college, a thing that women never do, or at least not the women who intend to become wives, and I was heavily in debt. I sat about aggressively in waiting rooms, waiting to be interviewed by banks, social-security officials and prospective employers, legs splayed apart, wearing a black mini skirt and sheer black tights peppered with ladders and holes. I wanted to be noticed. I was asking for it, up for it, out to get it any way I could.

Walters was the first man who offered me a job. He was the front man at the general office, supposedly managed by the agency. He looked innocent enough behind his barrage of telephones and his computer with a screen save of floating coloured fish, a gormless flotilla of shifting purples and greens. He sat very still, with his hands on the table before him. None of the pens in his little brown tray had ever been used. I noticed that. I remember thinking: there isn't a secretary. If this outfit had been for real, there'd have been a secretary, banging away at the order forms, memos and files of clients' desires. But there was none of that in this front office. This office is a stage set. This man does no work here. He's never written on that pad, never even looked at that calendar. He does it all through the computer. This man acts as front of house.

So I sat there, chewing gum and deliberately trying to look insolent. We eyeballed each other for a minute or so.

I didn't say anything. Neither did he. It's up to you to ask questions, mate. I could see that he already had me down as a cheeky bitch, the kind they bundle up and cart off every day. But I could also see that he didn't dislike me. He kept his hands folded on the table in front of him. Then he said,

'Stand up.'

I did.

'Pull up your skirt.'

There were only four inches of skirt to haul up above my cunt, but I pulled it right up to my waist anyway and he got a close-up eyeful of my shredded tights, my standard-issue black knickers, no lace, and the spiky pubic hair around my crotch. I don't shave like most other women do, or at least not like the women still studying how to be wives. Why bother? Why should I? Walters looked me over carefully.

'That'll do.'

I pulled my skirt down again.

'Turn around.'

I turned my back on him.

'Take off your T-shirt and bra,' he ordered, his voice utterly neutral and indifferent, as if he were asking me to find a file among the boxes outside.

I did as he asked.

'Now pick up the chair you were sitting on and raise it above your head.'

I was a little taken aback at this. The chair was made of iron tubes and plastic foam covered with a rough green surface. It was heavy and awkward. But I swim twice a week and I work out at the municipal gym. I keep fit. Really, it wasn't that difficult. I swung the chair into the air, setting my legs apart so that I kept my balance. The mini skirt creased up into folds around my arse.

'Hold it there.'

I thought he was going to walk around the desk and inspect the shape and fall of my breasts. After all, he would be paying me. I would be one of his girls. The agency has the right to have first look at the goods. But he didn't. I glanced over my shoulder and he caught my eye. But he hadn't moved. His hands were still folded on the desk before him. My muscles were beginning to shiver with tension.

'Two minutes,' he said calmly.

But it was longer than that. I must have held that heavy pipe-frame chair above my head for a full four minutes before I'd had enough. I swung round and slammed it down on the desk, dislocating one of the telephones and sending the computer mouse flying over the edge. The gulping fish vanished from the screen and my own face, sulky and shut, with all my basic details, appeared before me:

SOPHIA
DoB
Daughter of . . .
Present occupation: unemployed
Ex-student at Harrington Wives College
No siblings, one parent still living
Clean driving licence

'That's enough,' I snapped.

He didn't look at my breasts but at my face.

'Exactly so,' was all he said as he swung the computer round, out of my sight. I got dressed again without bothering to turn away from him. I was pissed off. He wasn't going to humiliate me quite so easily. I didn't give a shit about his fucking agency. I'd get another job somewhere else. Better paid. Maybe even in one of the international airports, or with the sex police, where you just took your clothes off or opened your legs, and where you didn't have to perform fucking circus tricks. I picked up my jacket off the floor and was about to stalk out when he said,

'Don't lose your temper. Sit down.'

I glared at him.

'You'll have to take the chair off the desk first.'

He hadn't moved. Don't play silly buggers with me, mate. But I decided to give it a go. I took the chair off the table and banged it down on the plastic floor. I took my time sitting down again. He waited. Not a muscle on his face was out of place.

'All right.' He smiled slightly. 'Let's do business.'

We sat staring at one another.

'I would like you to consider a position with us as a reception hostess. We will probably keep you in this country to begin with, but if all goes well I would hope to send you abroad for a year or two – either Germany or the Far East – to complete your training. I may be proved wrong, but it seems to me that you have the potential to be very successful in our line of work.'

I said nothing whatsoever. I didn't think much of his flannel. I was still pissed off.

'My name is Walters,' he said. 'You will be answerable directly to me.'

The first club in which I worked was called The Underworld. My code name was Cyane. Walters explained that I was named after a fountain in Sicily. I thought that it sounded very exotic. We all had code names. Some of them were very odd: Arizona City, West-world, Violet Gorilla, Dodge Kitty, Boudicca, Red Rita, Boy Cleo, Benton, Guido, Rampant Strap. The names were already attached to our identity discs. We were given no choice. I wondered if Walters had made them all up. Most of our clients were Japanese businessmen. You had to be a member, but it was possible to join at the door if you had a valid computer identity card and all the details, including the codes, corresponded to the citizens' identity database. That was one of my jobs as reception hostess: to run back-up identity checks on their discs to see if they were counterfeit, or if they were police, just visiting. If I found out that they were police I never turned them away, just pressed the Visitor's Button so that Walters knew the house was spiked that night and could make sure we kept the show nice and clean for the evening. That's not a problem. We just warn the boys and girls and they do routines that are within the limits. And for all the bloody bits we just run simulations.

We only had one raid that I knew about and that was the raid which closed us down: the infamous Jungle Show. We were even interrogated by the Race Police.

And that had never happened before. The Jungle Show was an old-fashioned scenario, very popular and passionately anticipated by our older clients, women and men – I never could detect a gender bias in their tastes. Our principal performer was a big black man with a handsome set of genitals. Huge, black and uncannily hairy. He did the whole thing in a cage with exotic flowering plants and a sound track of African drums and jungle cries. His partner was a young German girl, small, blonde, with large breasts. Her pubic hair was very dark. Walters didn't want her to shave, but he made her dye it blonde, which she told me took ages and stained her shower with yellow streaks, so that it looked as if she was given to urinating down the drain. But then, when he looked her over before the rehearsals, Walters suddenly changed his mind and told me to shave it all off. Her skin was very fragile and soft. I used a safety razor, but I was still terrified that I would cut her. She didn't speak much English. But I think 'Vorsicht! Vorsicht!' must mean 'Be careful.' And she kept saying that she was pretty pissed off with Walters. She maintained that he never knew what he wanted. In any case, old videos of the original act showed that the woman kept all her pubic hair.

I didn't bother with the rehearsals, although they appeared to involve an excessive amount of screaming. Well, if you work in the industry you lose interest in the soft acts pretty quickly. They're all much the same, and whether they're any good or not is up to the individual performers. But the Jungle Show, while classed as a soft act, aroused a lot of interest because it had the cachet of being illegal and first performed right back in the 1960s long before any of us were born. Walters came down to the dress rehearsal and decided that the cage should be suspended in the middle of the floor, just above the audience, so that the angles from which the show could be viewed were very exciting. He could charge more if the clients could see the action right up close. Walters is a showman to his fingertips. He knows what will make money and pack them in. Not that we could advertise any of it beforehand, given that the whole thing was illegal. But I knew the form. We'd done this before: make sure that the whisper goes round well in advance. That was my job really. I developed a sequence of euphemisms: a very special show, nothing like it seen anywhere in town for over seventy years, old videos, so very hard to get, a chance to see a real rave from the grave, and a hot night out. The clients get to know the codes. Everything I said meant that it was retro, illegal and violent.

One of the girls asked me why it was prohibited and I wasn't sure. So I asked Walters. By then we did have quite a good working relationship, even if he was a bit monosyllabic.

'It promotes hatred of black people,' said Walters, as if he had very little interest in the question.

I was mystified. At least half our clients are black. We were downloading the new computer information discs into our system at the time, and a quick glance down the list tells you everything: Ngato, Zwelo, Afrekete, Kabilye – they're all black names.

'Why should the Jungle Show do that?' I looked into the flickering green screen, still puzzled.

'Watch the dress rehearsal,' snapped Walters, indifferent.

I did, and then I understood what he meant. The show was bestial in the grand tradition. Our black star was presented like a gorilla in leopard skins with brutal, violent appetites and no imagination whatsoever. The act emphasized violence and fear rather than sadistic complicity, which is now so much the fashion. I prefer lucid, calculated sadism. It seems cleaner and more just. The German girl flung herself into her role. She played the victim all the way, right down to her shaved pubic mound. She cowered in the corners, tried to cover herself with foliage, and was absolutely convincing as a helpless abject prisoner, capping it all with one last, heaving, sweating gasp. But the performance was all about slavering brute lust, well out of control. Our black star presented a creature that was barely human. He was mere animal heat and priapic cruelty. I think that we were all rather shocked.

It struck me as odd that acts like this had ever been popular. I've never studied the sexual theatre of the mid-twentieth century and once I'd seen the Jungle Show, I didn't want to do so. But on the night we were sold out. All the clients were at least thirty years older than we were. It wasn't a market I had ever dreamed about. Yet they were all still there, shouting, gyrating and urging the players on as if they were massed round a bear pit. The public was every bit as raw and crude as the performers. I peered round the barriers from reception as often as I dared during the evening, to watch both the audience and the act. To me the Jungle Show seemed brutal, self-indulgent and lacking in nuance.

I'm a leather girl myself. So I enjoy the modern SM leather shows, orgies in the multi-user dungeon, with powerful roles for the women. I've never taken part in the show, of course. Walters always kept me either as front of house or circulating on the floor. I was his eyes and ears among the public. On the leather nights, however, he allowed me to dress the part. None of those soft, femme low-cut black dresses. No, I looked like the real thing: tight black leather suit, chains and studs. My only concession to femininity was a black leather rose behind my left ear. I always had offers on leather evenings. Not bad money either. Quite substantial sums. But private work was strictly forbidden. You negotiated your own salary with the agency. And some of the artists, not just the men, were very highly paid. I wasn't complaining. I earned just as much that night as the black stud in the Jungle Show. Walters used to say that I was worth it, what with my SM style and my computer skills.

On the night of the Jungle Show, when we were all nervous and tense, waiting for the off, Walters came downstairs. He told me to send the take at the door and the entire identity records straight up to his offices as soon as we had shut down the entrance and the show had begun. I was wearing a leather dress and my black rose. He added up the entrance bookings, plucked the black rose from my hair and then kissed my throat very, very softly.

'Well done,' was all he said, 'you've collected a very fine haul in your sexual net. You are my favourite domin atrix, the one that all the family can enjoy.'

I hardly recognized anybody who came into the club that night. I just checked their IDs, expressionless. And charged them the extortionate entrance fee Walters had dreamed up for the Jungle Show. The punters looked like pickled mummies. Some had stretched face-lifts and paint inches thick. The men were hideous, with folded jowls and savage eyes. I only remembered one of them, the one who withheld his ID chip. I stretched out my hand to receive the card and he closed his own over mine. I felt the chill of his heavy golden rings and looked up. He was huge, with a thick moustache and assassin's eyes. He must have been nearly sixty. His once dark hair was rid- dled with grey streaks. He was wearing an old-fashioned dinner jacket and a black bow tie.

'Just tell your boss that his guests have come.'

He nodded to my minders, dismissing us all. One huge hand was clamped around the elbow of the woman who was with him. In the narrow entrance to The Underworld, I looked straight into her face. She was afraid, terribly afraid.

Here was the frail, blonde face of a woman who lived in gracious spaces, surrounded by delicate, expensive things. She wore no paint at all. She was pale, her huge eyes dilated with apprehension and alarm. She was not here in this dark, permissive space of her own volition. She was not a free agent, as I am. She cannot have been more than eighteen years old. She was being forced. I looked at the soft lawn hiding her breasts. The dress was covered in thousands of tiny green flowers, embedded in silk. In this world of pounding, violent dark, she was a precious thing being dragged down, down, down.

I pressed the internal line on the com system.

'Walters? Your guests are here.'

'Thank you.'

He was utterly non-committal, quite unsurprised. I wanted to know who she was. I was wise enough not to ask.

The police turned up in force well after two when the show was nearly over. The German girl was bleeding from lashes and tooth marks on her arse and thighs. Her thrilling screams were perfectly genuine. She was begging the audience to help her escape from the cage. Our black player was quite crazed. I wondered if he was flying on coke. He was by now stark naked and his body was painted with red and black stripes which glimmered under the floods. The woman was tied up to a totem pole with her ankles in fetters, supposedly last worn by slaves. He was screaming about sexual revenge on the white tyrants. The audience was ecstatic. The woman was bent forward, bleating piteously. I wondered how much she was being paid and if Walters had made it clear that when we did retro, we went all the way. Verismo. Down to the last detail. We very seldom actually kill our performers, largely because the cost of the show, in security terms, puts it well beyond the reach of our usual clientele. There are specialist clubs for all that, but they're small, exclusive and have government security clearance.

When I next looked into the main house the black star was buggering the woman in a sequence of violent thrusts and the public were standing on their chairs, screaming. The cavern was filled with broken glass and smoke. I went back to the door and settled down with my usual thugs, checking the security zones on the computer. I saw them coming just a second or two before they crashed, roaring, through the door.

Police. All masked, heavily armed. One of them stuck a gun in my stomach and yelled,

'Get away from that screen, you fat bitch!'

I engineered a fall backwards, which gave me the chance to press the Visitor's Button. The thing is actually green, not red, and marked OPEN LAVATORY DOORS, one of our private jokes. I also managed to unplug the computer. This caused the entire system to utter a groan as it closed down. One of my bouncers took a swing at the officer pointing a gun at my stomach. Usually we don't attack the police, but he was taken by surprise. Nobody pulled the trigger, but three men fell upon him, pounding his chest and head with a mixture of fists and the steel shafts of their weapons. We could hear yells from the interior of the cavern, mixed with twentieth-century disco music, as the show was stopped short, well before the climax. I teetered up from the floor in my short leather dress and black high heels, pulling at my shirt, apparently in an attempt to make myself decent. As I did so I slid the information disc from the computer inside my knickers.

The discs are tiny, about the size of small coins, which used to be legal tender in this country, but have long since been discontinued. I planned to squeeze the thing up into my vagina and get rid of it before I was strip-searched. Police procedure is pretty standard. They usually search you before they let you go, on the grounds that what you take out of the police security zones is likely to be a lot more dangerous and more valuable than anything you could ever take in. The information on our discs is confidential and in the usual run of things clubs are not required to give them up. But we were, almost certainly, about to lose our licence. I had the real disc safely lodged in my most intimate crevices. The only list that the police could now find was the mail-order confirmation list, the names of people who had never stepped inside The Underworld in their lives and had probably never done anything riskier than order a leather suit, scented condoms and a silver-plated dildo. In fact, that list is littered with High Court judges, cabinet ministers and ecclesiastical dignitaries of every religious persuasion.

We were thrown into closed vans and removed in a cloud of howling noise. Walters was flung onto the same bench in the police zone waiting room. He thudded down beside me. He was remarkably calm. As soon as the officer in charge had taken all our details and drifted away, he leaned over and hissed in my ear,

'You have a handsome bruise swelling up on your left cheek, my dear. I assume you also have other things hidden on your person.'

'Well hidden.'

He nodded, then looked away. He seemed pleased, even slightly amused. He might have been smiling.

'Stand up, you smug fat cunt,' snapped one of the officers. 'You're spending at least one night in the cells.'

I was dragged away and I didn't see Walters for the rest of that night, or all the next day, or the night after that. I was locked up alone in a tiny graffiti-ridden cell with nothing but a couple of planks covered in a scratchy grey blanket. I was given no food and no water. There was a shit bucket in the corner, but nothing with which to wipe yourself. The floor stank of urine. I suppose the last inmate hadn't even been given a bucket. I'd been in prison before. I knew what to expect.

The graffiti gave me something to read. Some of it was antique and dated back to the period of the Jungle Show. There were peculiar historic slogans, like ONE NUCLEAR BOMB CAN SPOIL YOUR WHOLE DAY, YOU CAN'T KILL THE SPIRIT and, most mysteriously, PORNOGRAPHY IS THE THEORY RAPE IS THE PRACTICE. For us, pornography was like religion used to be, a condition of being, the way we thought, the way we earned our livings. And rape can't exist if all women, women everywhere, all of them, always say yes, yes, yes. I knew of no one who would think otherwise.

Walters himself came to bail me out. By the time he turned up, mid-morning on the second day, I felt humili-ated, smelly and cross. You can only go on pissing in the same bucket, when it's never emptied, for so many hours without beginning to feel disgusting. And I was terrified of losing the disc.

The officer who let Walters into the cell was the same one who had called me a fat cunt. My well-aimed gob of spit got him on the cheek while he was fiddling with his keys. He would have hit me if Walters, now dressed in an elegant camel suit with a long grey leather coat slung over his shoulders, had not caught his arm.

'I apologize on her behalf, officer. She is clearly desperate for a shower and a change of clothes.'

'Take your fucking clothes off,' screamed the man and banged the cell door behind him. Walters and I were left alone for a moment in the tiny cell.

'They will strip-search you before they let you go,' he whispered. 'Take your clothes off and give them to me. Give everything to me.' He met my eye pointedly.

'Didn't they get everyone in there anyway?' I started ripping off my clothes.

'The disc records everyone who passes through the doors.'

Walters held out his hand, irritated, urgent. Suddenly I knew that there were only two visitors who had not been hauled into the police zone: the green girl in her silken dress, covered in tiny flowers, and the man with the heavy rings of chilled gold.

Total strangers have seen me naked so many times that I have no difficulty undressing in front of Walters. He's one of the family. He had the grace to sniff the tiny disc appreciatively before slipping it into his pocket. Then he gathered up all my clothes, but held them at arm's length, suspended from his fingertips, while I trotted off to the shower, hugging my breasts.

A woman officer looked up my cunt and down my arse through one of those pencil torches with a magnifying eye at one end.

'What are you looking for?' I demanded smugly as she peered between my legs.

'Drugs,' she hissed.

★

The Underworld had been closed down. All the windows and doors had been boarded up with fibre-glass panels covered in yellow KEEP OUT stickers. I went round in the morning and experienced an odd sense of loss, standing in front of the anonymous brick block where I had worked for almost three years, five nights on, three nights off, six weeks holiday on full pay, when you didn't know what to do with yourself. The club was home now. I knew all the dancers, all the sex workers, all the live show players, all their regular animals, all the bouncers and security men, all the illegal transsexuals we used to employ off the books, and Walters, the boss. Our boss. He was standing behind me in the street, gazing at the anonymous shuttered door with THE UNDERWORLD in discreet blue neon, just above the arch and the descending staircase. The E was already disconnected.

I smelt betrayal and deceit. I turned on Walters.

'Why wasn't I questioned? Why wasn't I charged? Why are you and I free when everyone else is still in prison? You knew they were coming, didn't you?'

The sunlight catches the sheen on his hair. It is dyed. No man has hair that melting colour of red-gold. It is not natural. He is not natural. He is not even decent.

'My dear Sophia.' He takes my hand. I snatch it back. He shrugs. 'We are now considerably richer than we were three days ago and the police have hauled in an excellent catch, who could only have been dragged into the public glare by something as primitive as our Jungle Show. Of course the entire event was a put-up job. Credit me with some taste. Did you think I would have come up with a retro show like that as a commercial idea of my own?'

'And the rest of us?' I yelled. 'You may be considerably richer. The rest of us have lost our jobs.'

Walters gazed into the middle distance, somewhat displeased.

'Those of you who were up to scratch will be redeployed. But I will take this opportunity to shed a little excess weight. You, on the other hand, unless you have suddenly developed a social conscience, are more than welcome to accompany me to my new offices.'

I stood there in the washed sunlight of late spring, considering Walters' offer. He knew and I knew that I didn't have a lot of choice. In the old days women used to go to college and get themselves educated, just like the men do. There were many professions that accepted women, and not so many social sanctions on what you did. There were wives and whores, just like there are now. But those weren't the only choices. My mother's mother ran a taxi service: women drivers, women only. It's hard to imagine that now. She was married and earned her own money. Well, that's something that's no longer possible. You have to choose. You can either marry and never work, or work your arse off and live at risk. I saw how my father treated my mother, and how poor she was when he dropped down dead, and I reckoned I'd rather take the risk. I chose my life when I went to work in The Underworld. That's when my mother threw me out. No daughter of hers would ever work as a whore. And if you choose to train as a whore, my girl, out you go. But I'd done my sums. It's the only industry where you can make a packet while you're young – if you can keep your head on, and your nose out of the coke. I told my mother what I thought. But she still believed that respectable women shouldn't harbour whores in their houses. That's the line they plug on the Internet screens. She meant it. So did I.

There were plenty of runaway girls in The Underworld. Some of them crept back to their families when they lost heart. Others put themselves down on the Marriage Lists and were eventually chosen by men who didn't ask too many questions.

I sometimes wonder what it would have been like to be married. And when I think how much more comfortable and easy it would have been, I get a queasy feeling of regret. It didn't seem hard to choose to be a whore when I was twenty. It gets harder. Maybe being a wife gets harder too. The Work Palaces are full of redundant or runaway wives. Whores always have something to sell. Even when we're old. We starve less. That's a fact. It's a hell of a life, but if you make enough money you can buy yourself out and that's that. A place in the sun, well out of the way, in one of the desert countries, like Spain. You can't go on living in the north. Not once your ID has expired. Old whores never die. But they do tend to disappear. Never been to Spain. They say it's wonderful. Your own villa with a terrace and a pool, irrigated acres of oranges and lots of well-known criminals for company.

Walters is still standing there, waiting for an answer.

'How much?'

'Twice what you earned in The Underworld.'

'Done.'

I hadn't any choice, but this was too generous. Immediately I smelt a rat.

'What do I have to do?'

'Same kind of work. Some of it more confidential. See no evil. Hear no evil. Ask no evil.'

'So I've got to notice even less than I used to do?'

'Not necessarily. Just keep your mouth even more firmly shut.'

'And if I don't, I'll disappear.'

'Exactly so.'

Whores have no conscience. But then, neither do their employers.

'Well, that's clear.'

'I always am.'

He looked me over.

'But we shall have to shed this leather get-up and buy you some new clothes.'

★

And so I became front-woman, computer woman, tele-phone woman, wonderfully well-dressed woman, the woman with the manicured nails. I was no ordinary woman. I was the first woman anybody heard on the airwaves, or saw on the screen. I was therefore the first to meet Shaw.

I didn't even realize he was there. He walked in without knocking. I alerted security as a matter of course. No drama needed, not even a Visitor's Button. Just a gentle tap on the keyboard, as if you're bringing up the screen save. In fact, you do bring up the screen save at the same time, and it's fixed with the codes so that your work on the catalogue remains confidential while you are dealing with the emergency.

'Do you have an appointment?'

He shook his head and sat down. The camera eye swivelled round to record all his movements. Not that there were any. He sat down facing me, with his hands on his knees, and ceased to move. It's very frightening to be in the presence of someone who is utterly still. His features were unintelligible. If I had to describe what he looks like, I'd be hard pressed to get it right. He is like a stoat: very concentrated, very calm, then one swift gesture. Which is all he needs. That first time, I just looked at him and he just stared at me, cool as you please.

Then he said, 'There was no need to summon security. I am your new colleague. My name is Shaw.'

As the years have passed, my respect for Shaw has steadily grown. He is different from Walters. They are both quiet men, but Walters is always active, busy, engaged. Shaw has all the time in the world. He is like a professional undertaker. I do all the talking. Some clients call me the Cunt with Lip, but they aren't usually complaining. There were two aspects to our work, the front job, which was an ordinary sex agency, like many others, catering for specialist tastes, for upmarket clients, people in government or administrative branches of the state, and the dark side, the Special Jobs. These were not regular assignments and we always had very little time to prepare them. Sometimes they presented themselves like ordinary jobs. And I was only told at the last moment that this was a special. Like the first time. I think that you always remember your first time.

We had done a traditional dominatrix scenario in full costume. I still wore leather for work. And liked doing so. I had whipped him till he bled, shouting my usual graphic torrent of filth, which brought him instantly to orgasm. I quite enjoyed these jobs, as the client never touches you. That would spoil the effect. We were alone for hours. There was nothing unusual to report. Then I heard Walters calling quietly from the door. I ordered the client to wait and be a good boy or there'd be trouble, and stepped outside, puzzled. Walters never interferes. He lets me run my sessions any way I like. He knows that I'm a professional. But on this occasion Walters was very odd. He seemed tense, on edge, but he said nothing. He walked me out into the garden. I stood there, masked and naked in my long black boots. I began to feel uneasy, insecure.

Then suddenly I saw Shaw pulling the curtains in the living room where I had been working. I rushed back into the house.

The client was dead, his throat slit from ear to ear, his sperm drying in a small grim pool on the floor. But the slit throat wasn't the only mutilation. The corpse was disgusting. His entrails protruded from the sliced fat stomach and his penis, still unaccountably erect, poked at his flopping intestines. His blood oozed into the carpet. I felt sick and very angry. This was my first time, but I was already prepared to take pride in my work and to do a good job – thorough, untraceable. This bloated, repulsive heap was offensive on all counts. The work looked like that of an amateur, and very unconvincing.

Shaw stood by the windows, calmly cleaning his knives, without removing his black leather gloves. All the fluids and cloths he used were neatly folded and restored to his working case, which he then snapped shut. I stood before him, speechless with shock and rage. I pulled at my leather mask. It seemed to be nailed to my face.

'Oh for God's sake, clear it up,' I yelled at Shaw.

Walters was already addressing himself to our pocket computer, checking our emergency clearance. It came through in a series of muted beeps.

'You have half an hour,' said Walters mildly to me, as if we were going out to dinner. 'Go upstairs and wash.'

The client had never even touched me, but it was as if his blood was on my hands and thighs. The room smelt musky with the stench of fresh sex and violent death.

'Couldn't we do better than this?' I raised my voice. Walters looked at me carefully, then lit a cigarette.

'We were asked to make the death look like a ritual killing for the sake of the press, Sophia. Your rule should be to see no evil, hear no evil and ask no evil. I arrange the special assignments. I negotiate with the client. I assume responsibility and I do the research. This job, which you seem to find so untidily executed, has in fact been carried out in perfect accordance with our orders. I offer you and Shaw my warmest congratulations. Now do as I say and ask no further questions. I will excuse your outburst on this occasion simply because this was your first time.'

He would not excuse me again. I understood that at once. I stalked up the stairs and found myself padding across the thick pile in the master bedroom. There was a photograph of a pretty wife and three children on the glass dressing table. Where were they now? The client had been a family man. Most of them were family men. I shuddered at my masked face in the bathroom, then vomited into the sink. I had never done that before. When I peeled off the mask I found that I was shaking, not with distress for the bereaved family or horror that I had become an accessory to violent murder. The client was a politician. He must have sent many others to their deaths as a matter of course. No, what shook me was the fact that we were not what we appeared to be. I had imagined that we were an independent exotic sex agency; in fact we were assassins. The client was not the real client. Walters had described this as my first time. There would therefore be other times. And it had been so easy. He had called us up himself. I remembered sending him the catalogue, exchanging e-mails on the Internet, spicing up his appetite, upping the price. We had already been paid for his murder, twice over.

Now every client would be one of my potential victims. And I would not know the true nature of the transaction until Shaw suddenly moved. What I did for a living had radically changed. I would have no difficulty in doing it again.

On that night, as the black slick of our limousine cruised away across the hills towards our city, passing the checkpoints unchallenged, I felt the release of tension between the three of us. Walters let Shaw do the driving, which was unusual for him. Usually he drives and Shaw and I sit together, utterly silent in the back. Walters said nothing, but he took my hand and held it all the way back, down the steep ravines and across the gorges which separated the Heights from the city. I had no choice. He knew I had no choice. My future lay with them or nowhere. But even so, I willingly accepted the things I couldn't change. And there were obscure advantages. We were not ordinary people; we were the angel-makers, marketing sex and death as a gourmet speciality. I felt closer to Walters and Shaw than I had ever done. There were no longer three of us. We were becoming one person.

Intimacy is a peculiar thing. Between lovers it can show itself in a glance, in the caress of a cheek, in a whispered breath. But the intimacy between killers is a more subtle bond. We are each other's muscles, hands and eyes. In Shaw's silence or in the tension I can sense in Walters' shoulders, in the small of his back and the tendons of his neck, the crouched theatricality of our collective strength, everything I read from the pace of our breath, I feel my own force, my own arm raised. Lovers come together, separate. But we no longer follow that rhythm. My part of our bargain is never degrading to me, for when I tempt the client towards me, opening my arms, my legs, I feel the other two bunched in my stomach, my thighs, waiting. I am the first to go forward onto the dangerous ground, our killing fields. But I am never alone. And now I will never be alone. They are my guardians and my keepers, my cold eyes and my right hand.

★

The client wanted an ordinary, straightforward rape scenario: No. 2 in the catalogue – woman dressed not as whore, but as wife, lots of resistance, a bit of brutality, and then she loves it once she's forced. Then she's all over him, never known anything like it before, etc., etc. I've played it many, many times. Only the real sexual tossers ever order that one. Makes you wonder some-times. Walters gave me the brief without comment, but I noticed something, a rapid flicker in his gestures, the unnatural haste with which he fastened his briefcase, a glitter in his embrace. I scanned our orders. There was no mug shot of the client. He remained faceless.

'Who is he?'

'Ask no evil,' snapped Walters. Then he bent forward and kissed my nose. I had never seen Walters so thoroughly aroused. He was electric with anticipation. 'Dye your hair. Blonde. The client likes blondes.'

Walters knows him. So who is he?

But it was clear what manner of man he was when I saw where we were going, where he lived. We cruised up, up, up into the hills, luxurious in the leather and chrome of our limousine. Walters drove with ease and certainty. He knew the road. All the wealthy and the powerful live far outside the city. This man lived beyond the Heights. He lived on the slopes of the volcano. The view back down onto the plains was surreal, glimmering. The road curved above us into a landscape of darkness. We saw high gates, with ornamental grotesques grinning from the ironwork in the car's lights as we hummed past. The villas were all hidden in the trees. Sometimes the guards bathed us in searchlights, checking our registration. No one attempted to stop us. As we passed the checkpoints Shaw's hands, relaxed and open, never moved from his knees. He was completely concentrated. I began to feel sick. Someone was waiting. Our path had been cleared. I had never been driven into these hills. We were rising into the residential area occupied by the highest reaches of the government. I understood why I had not been allowed to know who he was.

I stared at Shaw's profile in the flickering dark. His stillness was absolute, unreadable.

When we reached the massive gates and the checkpoint with armed guards, Walters sighed slightly, and I saw that his hands left damp marks on the wheel. I looked up and saw two huge stone hydras stretching out their necks towards one another across the arch. All our papers and security IDs were checked again and again. We did not speak as the huge iron gates finally opened into the darkened gardens. As the car purred to a halt we heard water idling in the fountains. The great doors stood open against the warm night. The illuminated flags drooped against their masts in the windless air. Shaw vanished into the gardens, but Walters remained beside me. He carried his black briefcase. I stood hesitant on the steps, glimpsing the wealth of great spaces, parquet and carpets, cabinets filled with African masks and totems, an encyclopedia of cultures, collected under glass, polished, gleaming. The client was clearly erudite, cultivated. He owned hundreds of books. We passed from the great hall into the library. I saw a circular edifice of steps constructed to reach the topmost volumes. The room smelt of tobacco, long since obsolete amongst the general population. I recognized the smell. Only our most powerful clients still had the right to smoke. I could also catch the rich smell of spices: cloves, garlic, cinnamon. Who was he?

The palace appeared to be deserted. No servants bustled into the doorway, no animals scurried away. We stood patient, dark-coated, professional, waiting silent under the soft lamps. We were sombre as priests visiting the bereaved. No one spoke. Walters placed a chair in the shadows for me, then leaned against one of the columns. He did not appear to be surprised that we were forced to wait. Nearly an hour passed. Then one of the glass doors leading onto the inner courtyard opened and a shadow appeared in the doorway. I could see into the courtyard. It had a glass dome covering the roof, which was lit from beneath. The rectangle was overflowing with tropical and semi-tropical plants – hibiscus, bougainvillaea, lilies, cacti, palm trees – the inner garden was a micro-climate humming with the raw sounds of a tropical night and running water. A small gust of damp heat scudded across the hall from the open door.

'Come in.'

We advanced into a wall of humidity, an indoor green-house. I couldn't see the client's face, but he was wearing evening dress and smoking a cigar. He shook Walters' hand and there was a moment's displeasure, which I sensed, like a douche of cold water, as he looked me over.

'She's dressed like a whore. Send her upstairs. First floor, first left. Make her put on my wife's clothes. Then bring her back here.'

His voice was very calm, but had an eerie echo, as if he were speaking not from a place close to us, but from a long way away. I tried again to look into his face, but his features were always shadowed. Then I noticed his hands. He wore many cold, golden rings.

Shaw stood beside me. He touched my elbow gently and led me away up into the higher darkness of the house. Everywhere, I heard the trickle of running water. The interiors were very warm; fires were lit in all the grates, despite the mildness of the night. We entered a room of green mirrors. This was a woman's room, lavish as an Aladdin's cave. She had necklaces made with pure gold, pure raw lumps of gold, the gold you can only buy in the Indies, mined in the jungles. She had strings of black pearls and large brooches of onyx set in gold. He dressed her in black and gold. But she preferred green. All her casual clothes, T-shirts, jeans, her housecoat, her swimming costume – I pulled out drawer after drawer – green, all green. She had two entirely different wardrobes, one lavish and heavy, underwear, nightgowns, evening dresses, full length, all in black, edged with threads of pure, real gold. Her other clothes – I skimmed the racks – were light fresh cottons and raw silks, all in yellow green, bottle green, sea green, forest green, aquamarine green. And then I found the dress I had seen her wearing, a soft lawn hiding her breasts and thousands of tiny green flowers embedded in silk. I snatched it out of the cupboard and turned to Shaw, who was standing, unmoving, by the window, gazing out into the illuminated dark.

'Will this fit me? What do you think?'

He looked carefully at the dress. 'It may be a little tight. She is slighter than you, but the same height.'

'You know her. Who is she? Who is she?'

Shaw closed his eyes slightly.

'Put it on.'

I ripped off my leather suit and folded the green silk over my body. Her shape had been suggested by the dress. My own showed through, bolder, less delicate, unashamed. I sat down in front of the mirror and put on her jewels, all her green stones – jade, pearl and moonstones flecked with green.

I looked into the green-lipped shade of the mirror and saw again, superimposed on my own face, with all its lines of corruption and ambiguity, that pale fragile beauty I had known at once to be a precious, alien thing. She was not one of us, she came from somewhere else, somewhere across the mountains. The scent of her impregnated the dress. Her face flickered before me. She was here, somewhere in this room, watching my gradual possession of who she once had been. I looked round quickly, the long drops of jade caressing my neck with cold. No one was there but Shaw. He had not moved from the window, but he was now wearing his black leather gloves, his supple, working gloves, a second skin on his cold hands. He had shaved his head.

I felt the prickle of horror all along my inner thighs.

'Shaw,' I whispered, and he moved closer, his hands hidden. 'Don't let him touch me. I beg you, don't let him touch me. I couldn't. Not with this client. Do you understand?'

A tremor passed through his face, like a ripple in calm water. I had never, ever asked this before. Shaw, intent and still as a crouching cougar, simply lowered his eyes.

'Come downstairs now,' was all he said.

I stood up. The dress was long and loose at the hips, flowing outwards, rustling with her presence and the aroma of roses. I sensed the swaying raw silk billowing behind me. I felt taller, more graceful, as I descended the staircase. My steps echoed in the hallway. Her green slippers were one size too small for me, but I ignored the discomfort. It's not for long, it's not for long.

The rooms below seemed darker now; there were fewer lights. Walters had already vanished, and Shaw, who had begun to descend the staircase, was suddenly no longer there. I paused in the hallway, then stepped into the exotic garden. There were gravel walkways and everywhere, always invisible, the sound of running water. I examined the orchids, parasites cowering in the armpits of these heavy, lavish trees. Everything seemed huge, monstrous. The wet air clung to my face.

I heard his step on the pathway before me and then smelt his presence, tobacco and cinnamon. Now I could see his face.

I was expecting the grey-streaked hair, the killer's eyes and the heavy moustache. I remembered his cold, golden rings, crushing my hand, and the certainty of his authority. But he was not quite the same. Now the eyes were sunken back into the ancient face, the hair was thick, but quite white, the heavy face, white, cold, clean-shaven. He looked like a statue wearing a death mask. Layers of still fixity and cold thickened his gaze. He was as monstrous as his artificial tropics.

I had never been afraid of any of our clients. I usually see them at their most vulnerable, undignified, pitiful, pathetic. But this man was barely human. I was afraid of him. I staggered backwards and cried out.

His eyes glazed over into smoky white balls.

I had reacted precisely as he had wished.

Then he was on top of me. I felt a black rush of wings and heard horses' hooves, rapidly approaching. His dead white face was all that I could see. His hands were around my throat. I heard my own voice, far away, inside the echo of his snarl, screaming and screaming.

Suddenly the head snapped back. The world steadied. A red slit appeared in the monster's throat. The weight against me surged away, and I found myself sobbing hysterically in Walters' arms. He carried me into the hallway and set me down upon the last step of the staircase. I clutched the marble banisters. Walters reappeared with a glass of pure water.

'Here, drink this.' As I gulped it down Shaw stepped out of the tropical garden. He was unruffled, but his face was strangely drawn about the mouth. He carried no weapons. He was still wearing his black gloves.

'You take insane risks,' said Walters quietly. 'You moved too soon. Why didn't you wait? He could have killed all three of us.'

Shaw met his eye. He stood quite still, accepting the reprimand. Then he said,

'She was expendable as far as he was concerned. He intended to kill her.'

Walters paused, then nodded. He let his hand rest for a moment on my shoulder. I understood the gesture. There are three of us.

Walters closed the courtyard door without making a sound. He addressed himself entirely to Shaw.

'Where is his wife?'

'In the car.'

I looked up. We were taking her with us. Walters looked at the computer inside his watch. 'We wait another four minutes. Then we move. Can you walk?'

I could barely stand.

'My clothes?'

'Everything is already in the car,' said Walters.

I took off the green slippers and left them at the foot of the staircase. Walters leaned down and wiped my wet face with his handkerchief. He put his arm around my waist, as if I were an invalid, and led me out onto the steps and into the cooling night. Shaw closed all the doors behind us. The woman, dressed in Lincoln green, lay doubled up on the back seat. Her blonde hair gleamed in the dark.

'Put your jacket over her. Cover her hair,' ordered Walters.

I did as I was told. She was clearly drugged. The car surged away down the long drive, past the checkpoints. The soldiers showed no interest in our passing. We turned north, unchallenged, and headed towards the wild country. We had taken the opposite way to the one we had come. I sat wearing another woman's life along with her green silk and her jade earrings, while she lay, insensible, in black leather beside me. I could see the night world of open fields, little pockets of woodland, silent farms and cattle brooding in darkness, their white parts illuminated like a jigsaw with missing pieces. Shaw was driving fast. I overrode the computer locks and wound down the window, becoming calmer in the warm rushing air. I pulled my coat back from the woman's face. She was luminous, delicate, utterly beautiful. I gazed down at her still features, fascinated. Walters turned in his seat and watched me for a moment. Then he proceeded quietly with his instructions.

'In ten minutes or so we will reach the airport. Our plane will be waiting. Shaw and I will get out. Only a woman can complete the last part of the operation. No man is allowed to enter the sacred spaces. It is therefore your responsibility. You will find the directions on the car's computer. Follow them to the letter. You will take her to the appointed place and deliver her up to her mother. The place will be a little surprising to you, because there will be nothing to see but open land, vineyards and a grove of cypress trees. If she is conscious by then, simply turn her loose in the open. She will come to no harm. Her mother will find her. If she is still asleep simply leave her on the bare earth in the grove and come away. You are strong enough to carry her unaided. Your return journey will appear on the computer before you. You have just over two hours. So drive fast. We are not going back to the city. Our time there is now over. We are under new orders. We serve another master. On no account, whatever she asks, must you give her any explanations. You must say nothing. Nothing. Is that understood?'

I sat still, listening. Then I said,

'Can I keep her dress?'

Walters shrugged.

'That's up to you.'

He paused.

'Sophia, follow my orders to the letter. Give her no information. No information whatsoever. Whatever she asks and whatever you feel, say nothing.'

I nodded.

He turned back to the road.

★

I am driving, alone in the silent dark, when I feel her hand clutching my neck as she drags herself upright. She is warm, golden.

'Oh . . . Why am I here? Who are you? Who are you?' Her eyes meet mine in the mirror. I am following the red computer lights flickering on the dashboard before me. I do not reply.

'But I know you!' She is sitting up now. 'You are the reception hostess in The Underworld. The woman with eyes of pure blue water. You are one of my husband's creatures. One of his employees. Where is my husband?'

I do not reply. I do not react. I am under orders. I say nothing. She clutches my arm. I shake her off.

'Who are you? Who are you? Why have you done this? Why are you wearing my dress? Where did you find it? Why have I been imprisoned?'

I say nothing whatever. She is clutching the car door and crying. She is trying to escape. The automatic locks are in place. The car trembles and jolts over the gravel and ruts on the white road before us.

At last I speak to her.

'Is this your mother's house?'

The light shifts from black to dark blue. I see the olive trees becoming silver in the dawn. Before us are acres of soft green, fresh with the dew of early day. To the left there is a grove of cypresses, their dark, pointed shadows bolder against the light. Across the long slopes are acres of green vines. The goats' bells tinkle in the changing green shadows.

'Is this where you can find your mother?'

The car's computer tells me that we have reached the place where I am to leave her. And indeed I see nothing but vines, olives, and the whitening sky. She looks out at the landscape and then she howls, a long, unearthly cry of grief and longing.

'Pull yourself together. Is this the right place?'

The car's computer tells me that this is the right place. There is the little grove of cypress trees. I can hear running water and the rhythmic splash of a waterfall crumbling into a pool. I shall hit her if she gets any more hysterical. My nerves are on edge. I smell her husband's blood on my breath, my face.

'You know it is,' she whispers, 'but this isn't real, I cannot be free. I have dreamed so often that I am transported here. By some miracle. But I don't know you. I don't know how to thank you. Will I ever see you again?'

I do not answer. I have been ordered to tell her nothing. I have no answers to her questions. She strokes my arm with an appalling timidity. Her loveliness breaks over me. I look up into the tentative beauty of a woman whose life I cannot imagine, whose body sways with the fragility of spring. I belong to the unnatural world of concrete and darkness. We can never acknowledge each other.

'Who are you?' she begs. Who is it that she has to thank for giving her life back to her again? I cannot imagine. I open the car doors with an irritated click.

'Here, take this.'

Onto her lap I slam down the catalogue. She will finger it with horror. She will know us again. For we are imaged there, the creatures conjured from darkness to obey him. And there, folded into the glossy pages of daily perversion, directly over the orders of a man who relives his wife's rape for pleasure, again and again, is one name, our real name, scrawled in her husband's handwriting.

SOPHIA WALTERS SHAW

3

SMALL ARMS

It's funny how you can remember nothing whatsoever about most of the men you've slept with. Especially if it was only one night. And you'd had a lot to drink. Or your mind was on something else. Because unless they do something quite extraordinary, like licking you all over, or smearing your nipples with chocolate – or, oddest of all, talking to you and then listening carefully to what you have to say – well, it's not so much that you forget what they were called or what they were like, it's more as if they had never been there at all. You conjured them up out of nowhere, all by yourself. Imaginary lovers. Most women just imagine great sex anyway. Untrammelled, and on a plane. You have to. Otherwise you'd never get any worth mentioning. I used to masturbate while reading *Jane Eyre* when I was at school, but it's taken me twenty-five years to work out why Rochester is so sexy. After all, he's old enough to be her father, and she may not be Beauty, but he certainly is the Beast. Well, it's not the whips and boots, although that helps. It's because he talks to her. Really talks to her. And listens when she talks back.

I once had a boyfriend called Lange, while I was living in Köln. He was very tall. Lange means long. So he was. I can remember his car vividly. He had a Citroën Diane, pale blue, very dented and patched, full of bottles and rattles. He used to pick me up at dusk and we would hurtle round the cobbled streets with our teeth shaking. I don't really remember how tall he was. I am assuming that he was taller than I am because of his name. We used to smoke cannabis in the car. I remember that because it was extremely difficult to shave small pieces off the chunk and catch it all on the silver paper as the car bobbed up and down. Lange must have spoken German, because he was German. I speak German, so I must have spoken German to him. I just don't remember doing so. And I must have quite liked him, because I can remember the car. If I close my eyes I see the grimy dashboard and his large hand on the clutch in front of me. I see blonde hairs on the back of his hand. Then, if I glance down, I can see a mass of tools, tapes, tissues, fag ends, torn maps, dog-eared paperbacks, underground tickets and a postcard from Munich. It's of the Vier Jahreszeiten; all green domes and cupolas, with hushed carpets and silver trays. The kind of hotel where Gustav von Aschenbach would have arranged to have lunch with his publishers. But Lange himself? Did he have a student room? He must have been a student because he studied lecture notes, slept late and worked in a bar. But I don't remember him going to any seminars. I can't see the bed. I can't remember sex of any kind. I cannot remember his voice or his face. He was blonde, blonder than I am, because I remember using the wire hairbrush wedged on the shelf among the debris in the car and his hair was on the brush. And it was longer and blonder than mine.

I asked my mother about these strange black holes in my memory where faces and bodies should have been and she said not to worry, it was twenty-five years ago and you were stoned at the time. I said that I bet she could remember all the men she'd slept with and she said, well, yes she could, but that wasn't hard as there's only been your father. OK. So maybe I have more to remember. But that doesn't explain why everything erotic has the trick of vanishing. Well, maybe not quite everything. This happened twenty-five years ago.

★

I was looking at some eighteenth-century documents, housed in the state archive in Bamberg, West Germany. I was a young woman and the Vietnam war was still on. I was very interested in deciphering the Gothic script of the documents I was reading. I was enjoying the work. But I didn't have much money, so I was staying in a youth hostel. The youth hostel didn't have a bar or a games room, just a dining room, kitchen and dormitories with bunk beds and scratchy blankets. Most nights I was too tired to do anything except listen to German marching music on my trannie and then pass out. But on the last night in Bamberg I felt like going out. So I had a shower and walked half a mile down the road to a bar that didn't look too dangerous.

Bamberg used to have a huge US air base sited just on the perimeter of the town and enclosed by a massive wire fence. The camp was full of soldiers and there was a landing strip for nuclear bombers. QUICK TO

REACT said the sign in English. I turned the O of TO into a CND symbol one morning when I was waiting for the bus. I believe in graffiti. It's a form of free speech. Well, in those days the Wall was still up and not far off. The Russians were the enemy and they might be here any minute. And this time we were all ready for them. But the American soldiers who packed the bar weren't interested in the war. They were interested in bar billiards, English rock music and German beer. There was plenty of all three in the bar.

No woman who looks after her arse ever walks into a bar packed with men without looking around. The noise level was well over anybody's prescribed decibel limit, so I decided that I wouldn't stay long. This decision was influenced by the fact that I was the only woman in the bar. None of the men took any notice of me. I looked just like them, jeans, white T-shirt and military jacket, only my hair wasn't shaved to a razored fuzz. I sat down in a black corner next to the only other person in the bar who had long hair. This was a man in jeans, military jacket and round dark glasses. Where there should have been a double-barrelled label stitched to his jacket saying US ARMY and his name it just read KELLY. The US Army label had been picked off.

The barman appeared out of the strutting mass of men. He looked like Dracula, all black and white, surrounded by dense fumes of testosterone.

'Get her a beer,' Kelly commanded in Bogart English, without looking at me.

'Thank you very much,' I said primly. My mother told me you should thank a man who buys you a drink and then leave as quickly as possible, but not with him.

Kelly ignored me. He was staring at one of the other men playing billiards. Or was it snooker? Snooker is the game with lots of balls in a wooden triangle, like the Trinity, with added deities. The beer arrived. Kelly paid. I didn't say anything, just smiled and nodded like a plastic dog on the ledge of a car's rear window. Then Kelly delivered another Bogart-style line out of the corner of his mouth.

'See that guy with the shades? He thinks he's real cool.'

The Peter Fonda lookalike with small round shades was calculating his next shot at the balls from a variety of different angles, arching his bum over the table for the other men to look at. Cigarette hanging carefully at just the right angle, his movements were deft, exact. The hair on his arms shone in the smoky light. He was very sexy, and completely up himself. Yeah, he looked real cool.

'You're wearing shades,' I said sharply to Kelly. For the first time he swung round and looked at me.

Most men never listen to what you say, so they wouldn't have understood my tone. Women deliver a gentle feminine twitter, and if you're doing your girlie role right all you're trying to do is get them to talk about themselves. Now Kelly was trying, obliquely, to impress me by getting me on his side against another man. He'd bought me a drink and then he started telling me what to think. He was flying on automatic pilot so far as I was concerned. He wasn't interested in me. He was interested in the handsome soldier who looked just a bit like him. He wanted to be that man. You have to be committed to a very high level of pretentiousness to wear dark glasses in the middle of a bright crowded bar. Everybody did since *Easy Rider* had varoomed past on the screen with Jack Nicholson telling us all what liberty really is. But not everyone could carry it off. Kelly didn't look as good as the guy playing snooker. He looked tacky and used up. He wasn't fit. He was too thin. He smoked too much. He looked angry and sullen. But he was trying to look cool. He was trying hard. I had pointed out that he was trying too hard and that he wasn't winning. In those days I wasn't into telling men that they were wonderful. Especially not for the price of one beer. I was being rude.

Kelly got all that in one go.

'You a lesbian or summin'?'

'Yup,' I grinned broadly.

Kelly rationed out his smile. But it was a smile. One all. Serve to Kelly.

'Have another beer?' he asked pleasantly.

★

'None of these men have ever seen a war,' shouted Kelly. We were deep in conversation, but someone had increased the volume on the jukebox. I have never been able to work out how this is done.

'And you have, I suppose?' I yelled back.

'I was four years in Vietnam.'

'You aren't in the army now?'

I had demonstrated assiduously against the Vietnam war on numerous occasions, fled before water cannon, police cavalry charges and clouds of tear gas. I was quite prepared to do it all again, but by then even the US government didn't seem to think they could win. The Vietnamization of the war meant giving up and pulling out. I had assumed that, apart from the draft dodgers who got away, everyone else who went had been forced, more or less at gun point, to go.

'It's almost over,' I said, trying to sound consoling. Kelly at once understood that I thought he would be glad the war was lost and that the boys were coming home. His thin face turned white with rage. I looked at him, stunned. I simply couldn't believe that anyone could have been in Vietnam and come back believing in the war. But it turned out that Kelly didn't believe in the war. He hated the politicians and generals who had sent him out there to die. He hated his family who had held a party to celebrate his departure. He hated his father who had said how proud he was that a son of his was going out to fight the Commies in defence of God and America. He hated the women who had flirted with him and admired his uniform. He hated the sergeant who had hated all the new recruits as a matter of principle, called them 'ladies' and appeared to be little more than a paid sadist. But above all, he hated the draft dodgers who were worse than Charlie in the jungle, and the fucking peace brigade who had betrayed him. He therefore hated me.

Kelly's glare loomed out of a terrible cloud of smoke and pain.

'I was on the fucking base in Da Nang. I'm an engineer. I put the bombs on the birds. That's my job. I had good friends who got killed. Some of them got killed before my eyes. Fucking Charlie used to bombard the base every fucking day. We were like chickens sitting in a barbed-wire coop. We had nowhere to go. We never knew when the fucking rocket attacks were coming. You just sit there sweating fear. It can be daytime or night. In the jungle you can't see a fucking thing. Everything is too close. They're there all the time. Just watching you. One kid who worked with me – he came from Alliance, Ohio – I saw him blown to bits. I had his blood on my face, in my mouth. They sent me home for four months after that. But I walked round my home town where everyone thought I was a fucking hero and I felt like a ghost. I never said anything. I just drank and said yeah to whatever they said. I mean, what's the fucking point? And get this. I couldn't wait to get back to the base. It's as if nowhere else exists any more. I just put the bombs on my birds and sent them off every day, hoping that they'd burn a bit more off those fucking yellow bastards. That's all I fucking well did for four years. I'm the same age as you. Only while you were in college learning all your fucking poetry I was sweating and itching and yellow-assed with fear.

'. . . Sure I was fucking scared. I was fucking well going to die, wasn't I?'

Kelly hated everything and he no longer believed in anything at all. I searched through some of the fucking poetry I had learned and found Kelly in Shakespeare's *Measure for Measure*, drunk, imprisoned and well beyond all the limits of life and death. Arise and be hanged, Mr Barnardine. I'll not die today for any man's sake. Kelly was unfit to live or die. I took his hand in mine.

'Now you can get me another fucking beer,' was all he said.

★

Kelly talked on without stopping for over an hour. I said nothing whatever. I didn't even make the usual twitters and hoots women utter from time to time when men are talking. This wasn't a vain man boasting about his war experiences and demanding to be reflected at twice his natural size. I was on the receiving end of a quite breathtaking desperation. Sometimes he made no sense at all. Often he repeated whole passages, word for word, as if he had been hypnotized. Or he told me the same story, slightly differently, again and again. It was very strange. He was drunk, but not that drunk. He clutched my hand like a drowning man. The nearest thing to Kelly's discourse I have ever heard since then is Shane MacGowan and The Pogues. They both used 'fucking' as if it were a punctuation mark and their delivery is one long tuneless scream of rage and pain.

Suddenly he stopped. And all around us were cheerful, living, drinking soldiers and rotten rock music pounding on. I looked at the burning jungles, the vanishing bombers and the plastic bags full of dead white men.

I swallowed back the sick. This strange, haunted man sat before me, masked, blank, and trembling.

'Kelly. Take off those shades and look at me.'

He had terribly pale grey eyes and his pupils were vast.

'Have you ever told anybody else all that?'

The question completely confounded him.

'No. Should I've? You're English, aren't you? You can't tell fucking Americans. Apart from the fucking peace brigade, all they want to hear is how we're fucking heroes. I only talk to the guys from my works unit. And they already fucking well know. Every goddam fucking thing. Why should I talk?'

'Get us another couple of beers,' I suggested.

His step was steady, but his hands were ice-cold and shaking. We sat side by side, looking into the white heads of foam.

'You're my age. You left Vietnam over a year ago. What have you done in that time?'

He talked a little differently after that. He was calmer, more coherent, no longer submerged beneath his memories. He had gone to college in Alaska, because it was as far away from his folks as he could go and the place was empty, cold, remote. The people were taciturn and tight-fisted. The spaces across the forests and the lakes were huge. You could see for miles on clear days. In winter he travelled on snowshoes. He hardly spoke to anyone. He drank more than he should. He took drugs whenever he could get hold of them. He kept hearing the voices of men he knew were dead.

He was studying mathematics and philosophy. The maths was great, but apart from logic, philosophy was crap and he was going to give it up. He had no use for fucking Plato. Now he was contemplating dropping out. He had bought a gigantic motorbike. It's outside, he said, and he was touring Europe, which he had never seen. But in fact he always ended up near the American bases, drinking and scoring drugs off the soldiers in the bars, sneering at their naïveté and their clean, clean hands. For Kelly, there was nowhere else to go. The war would never end for him. It could never end.

The huge gulfs and chasms in my life now felt like minor shifts of gear compared to the horror of Kelly's memory.

'And who the fuck are you, babe?'

What version of your life do you give to a man whose mind is in shreds?

I described the landscapes I had seen, the country where I was born, the house in the hills that was my first home, my school, my college, my small student jobs, my vast ambitions and my idealistic politics. It was a narrative, small and pure, as fragile as fresh eggs. The candid pale grey stare absorbed everything I said. He did not let go of my hand. He was returning my compliment, and the intensity of my listening, my own suspension of judgement and disbelief. It took a while for me to get into my stride. At first, what I had to say did not seem important. What I had loved most, what I had lost. Only gradually did I realize that Kelly was listening to me with that terrible heart-breaking concentration of a child, hearing the magical fairy tale of an ordinary life, hearing it all for the first time and willing it to be true.

He listened without interrupting, and when I had finished he pounced on one thing.

'Hey, babe, you said they lied to you when they sold you all that crap about how being a woman was about marriage and motherhood. You didn't believe it. You didn't buy it. You refused to live your life just to suit someone else's fucking agenda. Feminists are all fucking dykes, aren't they? You're a lezzie, aren't you? Didn't you say you were a lezzie? Well, they sold me a fucking load of lies too. About God and America and the mother-fucking Communists. The whole damn shit-pack of goddam fucking lies.'

This was delivered with astonishing, affable good humour and satisfaction, as if something had been revealed to him. He squeezed both my hands with real affection. We'd been conned, but we'd seen through all manner of conspiracy. In a blaze of beer and truth we gazed at one another, Tobias and the Angel, exploding with prophecy. We couldn't get through whole sentences any more and it was well after one in the morning. We had talked without stopping or letting go of each other's hands for over six hours.

The bar had emptied out. The jukebox was silent. The soldiers were vanishing in gusts of male laughter. The landlord and the barman were packing the glasses onto the bar. The ball was over.

'Where're you staying?' I stood up, stiff and a little cold.

'With you,' said Kelly, pulling a beat-up leather jacket and a sleeping bag pack out from under the seat where we had been sitting.

I laughed.

'I'm in the youth hostel down the road. There are boys' and girls' dorms,' I said pointedly.

'I'm sleeping with you, babe,' Kelly replied mildly.

Our beer bill amounted to fantastic sums. The landlord accepted Kelly's dollars. For once, I let the bloke pay.

And so we staggered away down the road in the dark, clinging to the kerb. On the other side was the high wire mesh of the fence around the base. All the lights in the hostel were off, and the door was locked.

'You gotta fucking night key, babe?'

'No, I haven't and don't keep calling me babe, you patronizing sexist bastard.'

Kelly chuckled all the way back to the bar. By this time the landlord was locking up. Kelly offered him another fistful of dollars. He refused them, but told us we could sleep on the floor in the bar. Kelly laid down his coat and sleeping bag on the smelly, sticky floor with a graceful flourish, worthy of Sir Walter Raleigh, and we lay down together, quarrelling good-humouredly until we fell asleep, like two tumbled kittens, in one another's paws.

Next morning, the landlord woke us at seven. Kelly's leather jacket was cold against my mouth. I smelt stale beer on his breath and in his hair.

'Ugh,' I said, 'you need a bath. You're disgusting.'

He looked paler and thinner in the morning light.

'You've got a fucking hangover, babe,' he muttered amiably, lighting the first fag of the day.

I saw Kelly's bike, which was parked outside the bar, for the first time. It was the size of the Sphinx, with two gigantic silver exhaust pipes and wing mirrors on stalks. It looked like a killing machine. I have always wanted a motorbike. My mother never let me have one. Kelly appreciated my envious glance and put his arm around me.

'You get yourself a fucking bike, babe. All the dykes in LA have bikes. And tattoos. You could get yourself a tattoo at the same time.'

We marched back down the now busy road to the youth hostel, shattered, yellow-eyed and stinking. The youth hostel was open and the censorious, hatchet-faced woman who had told me to turn my music down even when I was the only one in the dorm, was sitting in the glass box. She glared at me.

'Sie müssen Ihr Zimmer sofort aufraümen, Fräulein. Aber sofort.'

'What'd she say?'

'I've got to clear up and leave.'

Kelly nodded insolently at her and marched off towards the stairs beside me. The woman leaped up, popped out of her glass box like a circus trick and let out a torrent of outraged Deutsch. On no account could Kelly enter the building.

'They don't like you. You been here before?'

'Tell her I'm going to carry your fucking suitcases,' snapped Kelly from behind his shades.

'Er will meine Sachen tragen,' I said, not very convincingly. Then added, for effect, 'Er ist ein Gentleman.'

Kelly glinted evilly. The woman glared back. We rushed upstairs and locked ourselves in the shower. I used Kelly's shampoo and he used my soap. We scrubbed assiduously at our hangovers and saturated all the youth hostel towels out of spite. An hour or so later, washed, combed, and in cleaner clothes, we confronted the bike. I only had my small rucksack, which fitted easily into Kelly's massive saddlebags, but he didn't have a second crash helmet.

'Just keep your head down on my shoulder, babe,' he suggested, 'and maybe we'll get away with it. Where do you want to go?'

'Nuremberg.'

Kelly looked at the map and memorized the route with uncanny accuracy.

'Nuremberg. Wasn't that where the last fucking war ended?'

'Sort of. It's where they tried the war criminals. Wars never end.'

Kelly nodded and clamped an opaque black visor over his face. Once on the back of his monstrous engine I was raised slightly above him, catching the wind full in the face. So I crouched down as the bike roared away, holding him tightly round the waist.

The roads between Bamberg and Nuremberg are very beautiful, forested, wheatfields, the odd little lake shining in sunlight, immaculate villages peppered with pots of geraniums and super-white, flower-patterned net curtains. I saw this rural idyll flash past in glimpses as my eyes were clenched tight shut and my mouth was open in one long terrible wail of fear. Kelly had lost all fear of death since his escape from Vietnam. But he was now clearly intent on killing us both. I screamed and screamed and screamed. Kelly heard nothing. I tightened my grip on his body like a maniac, bent on murder by hugging. It made no difference. Kelly leaned into the curves and we fled through the thick summer light like gaolbirds on the run. He occasionally paused at the lights, but by that time I was weak with fright and the repetition of the rosary. I thought I was still screaming, but in fact I was just whispering, stop, stop, stop. Kelly patted my clenched white hands with a black leather glove and shifted a little to loosen the tightening clamp of my arms around his ribs. Inside the helmet he was locked away from the world. It was his mask, his other face.

We reached Nuremberg by midday. Kelly's bike bounced over the cobbles up to the very door of the next youth hostel and all my teeth were rattling in their sockets. He balanced the bike on a slender silver peg and waited for me to crawl stiffly off the beast. Kelly paused, lifting the opaque black mask from his face. Amazingly, he was wearing his shades underneath. He must have seen the bright landscape as a sequence of frozen black masses.

'What's the matter, babe? You nearly cracked my fucking ribs.'

'I was scared,' I mumbled feebly, collapsing on the edge of the pavement.

He was very concerned.

'Scared? You shoulda told me to slow down.'

Short of biting his leather shoulder, which he would probably never have felt anyway, there had been no possible means of communicating from the back of the bike. Cracking his ribs had been the only alternative left.

'Forget it. We're here safe.'

He looked at me. I looked at him. He took off his shades and we stared at each other. We both knew that we would now say goodbye and that we would never see one another again. How do you deal with these moments when the script gives out? You see, with men and women there's always a script. You just wait till the moment comes, get your expression right and say the lines. You can learn them by heart off the movies. There are scenarios for every situation. There was even a script for our moment. But one crucial detail was missing. If it had all gone according to the director's plan we should have screwed each other senseless in one single night of passion, then parted for ever, filled with tender memories and regrets. One long, lingering kiss. Music. Cut. THE END. Credits roll. But Kelly and I were facing one another, dry-eyed, knowing that we had spoken our piece – no scripts – just what we had to say, and been heard. We had come to no understanding, no agreement; the dialogue was still there, open-ended, but the quality of our attention, clouded by beer rather than lust, had all the disconcerting drama of a one-night stand with the peculiar, unending intensity of family relationships, where the connection between you is written on the walls, in your faces, in the past behind you and in your hands round the glass.

We stood staring at each other, trying to possess every detail of the face that was already fading. He leaned forward and kissed my cheek gently. He smelt of soap – my soap – old leather, engine oil and petrol.

'So long, babe. Get what you want the first fucking time around. And have a nice life.'

Well, that was the kind of thing we said then. That was our script.

'Goodbye, Kelly. Thanks for the ride.'

He replaced the visor and his face vanished. Then he swung back onto the bike, which had been purring noisily beside us, and rolled away down the cobbles, collecting German glares as the exhausts sputtered forth the odd black cloud. At the corner he hesitated, one leg lowered on the curve. Then indicated left and swung out into the slow traffic.

'Go back to Alaska and get your fucking degree,' I yelled at his black leather figure, retreating for ever down the green roads. I'm quite sure he never heard me.

*

No, I never saw him again. Not from that day to this. We're the same age. Where is he now? Fat, middle-aged, living in a condo with shared lawns, a bitch of a wife and two kids? Or is he a civil engineer in a big firm, ordering other people about? Did he ever go back to Alaska and stay up there in the white wastes and forests, never visiting a sweaty, brilliant climate again? Or did he go back to the US Army, the only family he had? Would they have had him back? What is the last place left for a man whose life has been stolen from him? I think of him every day. Odd, isn't it? He never even asked my name.

Have I had a nice life? Pass. But of one thing I'm dead certain. I never did get what I wanted the first fucking time around. Nor the second time. Does anybody? Maybe the trick is to know what you fucking well want and to stay in control of the plot of your own life. To put the matter as Kelly would have done.

I worked, spent money, drank more than I should have done and took drugs whenever I could get hold of them. I kept hearing Kelly's voice.

Well, what's changed in twenty-five years? Mass unemployment for one thing. Gone are the days when I worked at well-paid jobs for as long as they interested me, handed in my notice when I felt like it, blew most of my salary in the clubs over one weekend, slept it off Monday and got the next job on Tuesday morning. I used to do that. Incredible, isn't it? Now I keep my head down and my mouth shut. We might mutter in the lavatories, but we aren't going to put our bloody heads over the edge in a meeting. Working hours for the poor sods who've got jobs have doubled since then, and if you've lost your job you might as well take to drugs and crime, because sure as we're all going to die, you're never going to get another one. I turned slick and cynical to suit the times. But I did keep on hearing Kelly's voice. And I kept on hearing all my own self-righteous crap, which I used to pour out over anybody who'd listen. And even over all the people who tried to avoid me.

We had a very evangelical streak in those days. We were always trying to convert everyone else to our point of view. One of my girlfriends told me that she'd always been convinced that deep down, if you got someone talking and they really opened their heart to you, they'd admit that they were secretly revolutionary socialists who wanted to eliminate hunger, poverty, injustice and oppression. Think again, sister. What we all want now is more money. And I'm no exception. I even watch TV programmes about alternative investments. A girl has to have a bit put aside for her sell-by date. We've all got more litigious, too. It's a creeping disease from the USA. A couple of us at work are collecting information on how to sue your employer if he works you too hard and your health gives way. We're all warm advocates of Victorian values, Darwinian survival solutions and the cash-nexus.

Even the wars are high-tech now. Just lock on with your computer-adjusted target screen, press the button and blow 'em away. We're still killing people with impunity, especially civilian populations. Look, there they go, felled by machete, machine-gun and precision bombing. Even barbarism is quite fashionable: shrunken heads on stakes and kinky rituals, children starved to death in cellars by Internet paedophiles. Real heart-of-darkness stuff for the nouveau *fin de siècle*. Hell, the whole world was just as fucked up twenty-five years ago. But we felt like we could do something about it. We thought we could change things. Some nights, when I feel particularly alienated from the whole damn circus, I dream of a man, coming towards me, carrying a black plastic sack and a rake.

Eventually, many, many years later, long after any normal person would have forgotten that night with Kelly, I decided that I needed a very expensive holiday, paid for by someone else – travel, hotel, meals, the lot. So I went on a diet, bought some slick new clothes, had a makeover and picked up an idiot called Charles, who liked talking and needed someone who would give him the impression that she was hanging, thrilled, upon his every word.

Charles was rather good in bed, but deathly boring when he talked. That's true of many men, isn't it? My aunt told me about one of her Italian lovers, who was a count, but very wicked and indeed, a Fascist. How could you have stayed with him? I demanded incredulously. He was terribly good in bed, she said. Sex blinds you to everything else. But Oh dear God, he was boring. Did you know that Fascism is boring? And even if he talked in bed, lovey-dovey conversations to urge you on, he was boring. But it's what men say about women, too, don't they? Well, said my aunt, they must be looking in the glass, and seeing nothing but themselves.

So I slept with Charles on and off for a couple of months and listened, thrilled, to everything he said. Then he suggested the very expensive holiday.

I got the impression that he was a university professor, and then, very oddly, that he sold international telephone systems. You see, I am excellent at giving the impression of listening, thrilled, to every word, and I always absorb enough for the odd, coherent comment, but I don't ever pay one hundred per cent attention. Wouldn't be worth your while now, would it? I grasped that Charles liked doing other men down and then scoring points off them. But at first they appeared to be university colleagues in his own and other departments and then, later, men who represented other companies. Time to ask a discreet question.

'Was that at the university?' I queried the steady flow.

'No, no. Much later. I was better off in industry. No profits to be made out of being a research professor in Communication Studies. In the university I earned £53,000 a year. No one can live on that kind of money.'

No, indeed not. Mystery solved.

Charles never asked about my past. He asked whether I had any money invested, and when I told him how much and where he rang up his broker and worked out a much better deal for me. This was very kind of him. This was the kind of thing he did. He thought I was rather interesting in bed and asked me where I had learnt how to do it. I told him I had been initiated into the secret world of Suzy Wong by Suzy herself. And then expanded upon the theme of what lesbians do in bed, which turned him on no end. Amazing, isn't it? That they have to be told what we do. It demonstrates not only a pitiful lack of imagination, but also a quite fantastic ignorance of female anatomy. I recycled all the descriptions in *Fanny Hill,* as I was absolutely certain he would never have read it. Books are useful in emergencies. In fact, I'm convinced that I could have recited most of the heterosexual sex in D.H. Lawrence and Charles wouldn't have recognized it as heterosexual – or even as sex. He did Business Studies at college, which appeared to be a mish-mash of accountancy and law, and all he had ever read was the *Financial Times* and the *Wall Street Journal* on the Internet, back issues in microfiche. For pleasure he read theatrical and cinematic biographies and was under the impression that everyone involved in the Arts was a pederast.

Now I know what you're thinking. How could she so shamelessly betray women's secrets? And how could she sleep with a man she despised? Well, dears, very easily. Most women sleep with men they despise. Most women will say that they love men they despise. Get any married woman drunk and ask her. We don't cherish many romantic notions. Especially if we don't have an income. Mr Rochester was quite right. When Jane Eyre lets fly one of her little bursts of self-righteous cant about the freeborn refusing to submit to humiliations, he rightly points out that the theoretically freeborn will submit to absolutely anything for the sake of a salary. I have held down a sequence of quite unspeakable jobs and know this to be true. And after all that, hotting up Charles before one of his magnificent performances seemed like doing a harmless turn on *Blue Peter* for the benefit of the kids. Anyway, I didn't really despise Charles. I rather liked him. He had his advantages, which I'll enumerate, all in good time. I just had very low expectations of what he was capable of understanding. And as for women's secrets, lesbian sex isn't one of them. Have a glance at any soft-core porn mags on the top shelf in your newsagent's. It's all there, in graphic detail. They know what we do and what we look like with all the paint scrubbed off. One thing they don't know, and will never know, is what we think.

Charles bought a new BMW especially for the holiday, with state-of-the-art CD equipment and the very latest in telephone technology. I rang my mother from the car, just before we rolled down into the Channel tunnel. She was very impressed.

'I like the telephone system,' she said graciously, 'however, I do wish you would give up that idiot.'

She wasn't impressed by Charles.

'He's right here beside me,' I said, 'looking wonderful. And he sends you his love.'

Which he did. Charles looked very complacent and fabulously dressed in Ralph Lauren and Calvin Klein finery, right down to his underpants. He looked like an extra on the set of a shopping-and-fucking film. I always thought it was a pity that he wasn't homosexual: another man would have appreciated the elegance of his dress sense more convincingly than I could.

On with the holiday. Tourism is one of the most irresponsible things you can possibly do. I read a magazine for Francophiles called *France*. It's incredible. An entire country of beauty spots and gourmet cooking. Lying open like a fresh clam, waiting for you to fish out the flesh and consume. You don't have to think about poverty, unemployment and homelessness. Join the well-off middle classes. Pick your route according to the mag and cruise down sunlit, poplar-lined roads, spotting the odd rustic peasant joyfully engaged in timeless rural pastimes, untouched by the EEC subsidy. In every *auberge* the smiling, ruddy hosts propose fabulous menus of five courses or more, *vin compris,* that are excellent value. Try our local aperitif – Calvados in Normandy, Pineau in the Charente, Pastis in the Midi – fill the boot with wine. You don't pay tax on quality and anyway, you've paid the VAT. The French have been told to love the tourists and welcome you with sinister friendliness. Cruise on down past the Dordogne, and the solid stone barns selling the wines of Cahors, the RN20 carries you along the edge of the Massif Central, superb views to left and right, sail over the little hills that let you down gently into the white-hot light of the south. And you're there. *Enfin, en vacances.*

Charles went on holiday to have sex and to talk and eat in between the sessions. What I could appreciate was the sex. He was one of those men who talk you through the initial manoeuvres as if he was dictating instructions to his secretary. Lift your other leg slightly. Turn onto your stomach. Gently does it. Mm, isn't that nice? I know it sounds peculiar, but in fact it all unfolds quite surprisingly. Your body is rediscovered every time, announced like a train, as it arrives on the threshold of orgasm. Why, here we have two nipples – good heavens sir, erect – and here a belly, pleasingly flat, with a pretty little well in the centre, a fine, delicate line of fair hair descending to, well, a darker, crisper little grove, neatly shaped. Have you ever considered topiary for your pubic hair? Maybe your initials? Or better still, mine. And here the deep romantic chasm with the peeking clitoris, blushing pink with pleasure.

Charles's favourite picture in the Musée d'Orsay was a graphic split beaver, painted by Courbet for a private collector and entitled, of all the hypocritical nonsense, *L'Origine du Monde.* I went back to see it recently with one of my girlfriends. She attracts nutters for some reason neither of us can account for.

'He liked *that?*' she demanded, incredulous.

'Yup,' I said, grinning. 'He thought it was a work of genius.'

'He deserved all he got,' she said, grimly.

The inevitable American nutter cruised up to us.

'I think that's beautiful. I sent it as a Christmas card to all my friends last year.'

'We think it's pornography,' we squeaked in chorus and fled away, muttering, before he could put us on his Christmas card list.

But to do Charles justice, he wasn't only keen on the peeking clitoris in paintings. He liked the real thing. Most men don't actually like women's bodies. They're jelly-like and ooze slime. But Charles did. He was all for a tongues-on technique and was bitterly disappointed if he ran out of breath and was forced to come up for air, his face drenched in juice. I was in for a good holiday and great sex. Women have always sold sex for food and board. I was actually enjoying the exchange. So point the finger if you dare.

Whenever we got to the hotel we did the same thing in the same order. Shower, sex, shower, dress, dinner. Day after day after day. On the night it all happened Charles had first turn, second round in the shower and was sitting up in the window seat against a background of geraniums, immaculate in white raw silk, reading about the local restaurants in the guidebook. I emerged from the pink marble bathroom, dripping, glowing.

'How about this one? L'Auberge de la Croisade. *"Sous une terrasse ombragée, au Bord du Canal du Midi, l'Equipe de l'Auberge de la Croisade vous proposera ses menus avec leurs spécialités régionales et gastronomiques."'*

Charles speaks excellent French, much better than mine. This is part of his allure.

'Sounds good. Like to go? It's got two stars.'

You choose, I thought, you choose. You will anyway.

You know how your mind drifts when men are talking about themselves? It isn't that you may as well not be there. Actually, you're essential to their discourse. You're there as a sort of glowing swamp, sucking up all their minor victories and radiating admiration and approval. My experiences have led me to believe that they don't care if you daydream while they're fucking you, but that they lose their rag at once if they find out that you weren't listening. Well, here we are, installed at our corner table in the Auberge de la Croisade, well into our seafood entree and my mind is wandering, but my expression is carefully in place. Don't eat too fast. It's then too obvious that you haven't said anything, but that you've managed to finish all the oysters.

It was well after nine o'clock and the great summer light shifted from white to pale yellow and now began to breathe out a peaceful, delicate shade of pink. The trees shuddered in the first faint breeze of the day. The table-cloths rustled a little in the warm wind. The napkins on the few empty places stood up stiff, like bishop's mitres in their glasses. All around I heard the ebbing gust of talk at the tables.

An appalling French family, diagonally opposite to us, had begun to disintegrate as an eating machine. The two youngest children were now roving among the tables, firing at one another with a variety of plastic gadgets. The youngest trod on a small dog that was buried in and around its owner's handbag. The dog yelped, then snapped at the boy's ankles. The owner snarled at the mother of the cruising plastic terrorists, who replied that it was up to her to control the dog. I was amused by the injustice of this and wanted to laugh, but Charles, who had his back to the main body of the restaurant, droned on, not noticing the incident.

'. . . Well, of course it was out of the question to go on with the flotation. So we pulled out of the market. We just withdrew the shares, after three days. I took full responsibility for the decision.'

One of the would-be terrorists now had on a mini-ature military vest with pouches for ammunition and folding knives. This was too big for him and caught on the chairs as he dived behind them. The children had both begun to make takka takka takka noises as they obstructed the waiters. One of them had allowed his fixed rictus to slip and he was now glowering at the scampering children.

'. . . one of the essential elements of management, knowing when to delegate and when to take on the full burden of the company's future. It is, after all, in my hands, and we now have nearly three hundred employees.'

Navarin d'agneau. What a sauce! *Pommes de terre dauphine.* Fresh green beans, very delicate, all the same length. And the wine, made by the local mayor, whose *domaine* you can see from here, no, to the left, that big estate with the umbrella pines, circling the gateway, carries the hallmark A.O.C. St Chinian. Some more red, darling? It's delicious. Smile slightly. Don't wolf it down. There'll be more of this tomorrow. Why do you always eat as if you were starving?

But I had begun to hear another voice, a faint echo, cradled by the years, safe in the past, but louder and clearer than it had ever been, telling me what it was like to live with no meaning or control, to be among that class of men who have no future, whose lives are in the hands of other men.

'. . . there are other lines of development possible for the company. There's no need to regard this as a defeat.'

What is it like to know that your life has no value? That the men who hold your life in their hands think that life is worthless, expendable.

Takka takka takka.

'Tu es mort. J'ai tiré.'

The children knocked over a chair. All the glasses on the table rattled precariously against each other. Their mother rose up and started shouting. There was a universal, ominous pause in the restaurant's conversation. The terrorists were banished to the terrace, where they fired on a terrified ginger kitten and then began, systematically, to destroy a row of bold red geraniums.

It stinks, babe, it fucking stinks.

Kelly.

'. . . there's a war on. A telephone war. And there are going to be casualties.'

The fields were filled with an uncanny pink gleam, rising from the earth. I watched the waters of the canal darken. A long way round the flat curve of still water I could see the lights of a barge moored for the night. Two cyclists followed by a panting labrador whirled past, jingling and laughing, vanishing behind the reeds, down the canal path, into the warm cavern of pink light.

Where are you, Kelly? Where are you now?

'. . . it's up to me to make sure we're one of the winners.'

Ruthless fucking bastards.

'What did you say, darling? Ruthless? Well, that's a bit strong. But uncompromising, tough, yes, you have to be. The competition is pretty stiff. We aren't the only ones in the field and we're also not the first. Our product has to supersede what our competitors are offering. But we have a lot more possibilities in the Third World . . .'

Takka takka takka.

All the geraniums had been subdued. The terrorists were negotiating a sequence of table legs, darting from one to another.

The light was changing again from that shell-pink, delicate as the inside of a female conch, to a deep, darkening blue. I saw the headlight of a single bicycle coming towards us, along the towpath on the other side of the canal.

The French family were ordering cheese and ice cream. The children laid their small arms on the table, pulling at the menu and shouting exuberantly. *Moi, je . . .* I, me, my, more.

'What would you like, darling? Tiramisu? Or *tarte aux abricots maison?*'

Charles studied the menu.

You choose, I thought. You choose. You will anyway.

I had a better evening blind drunk in a bar in Bamberg with a man I never saw again. Those were the days when I had no money and wore tight blue jeans, a white T-shirt and a military jacket with the labels picked off. Those were the days when I hitchhiked around Europe on my own and cursed rich fucking bastards like you when they drove past and didn't pick me up. Now I ask you, do I look like a rapist, a murderer, a terrorist? Takka takka takka. We used to aim our imaginary machine-guns at your tyres.

Je veux pistache, vanille.

Green. White. *Je veux.*

'Why not have the apricots? Tiramisu is very rich, isn't it? And you're watching your waistline. Can't have you filling out at this stage.'

I smile brightly and agree.

The cyclist has stopped on the bank opposite the restaurant. He has his back to me. He is a young man with long hair and a green jacket. He is unpacking a large basket, which is perched on the back of the bicycle. He is a fisherman setting up the evening's peaceful watch. Isn't he a little late? Are there fish in the canal? Do Frenchmen fish at night?

The French children are banging their spoons on the table in turbulent, unholy glee. The Dogwoman has called for her bill. She has had enough of the rumpus. Disapproval glitters in every line of her sleek chic suit. The dog, impeccably behaved, has extracted himself from her handbag and is leaping up, placing his paws on her thigh. She pockets the silver chocolate square she had with her coffee. For later on.

'And I'll have the chocolate gateau,' says Charles, smug with satisfaction. He wipes his handsome lips upon the napkin.

'Even the better places in Soho give you paper napkins now,' he adds regretfully. 'One of the great pleasures of travelling in France is having linen napkins. Even a rural auberge like this one. Really very good value.'

He looks down the menu.

'More wine, dearest?' He is contemplating a *petit alcool*.

I smile even more brightly and place my glass close to the bottle. A revolution breaks out at the other table when one child has two scoops of ice cream and the other has three. The waiter begins to negotiate amidst the shrieks and cries. The children pogo their protest, standing on their chairs.

But out of the corner of my eye I see the white face of the young fisherman staring at us from across the canal.

The restaurant is still full. In the huge jumble of voices around me his white face is a still point of silence and concentration. Then he bends down and begins assembling his equipment, which is spread out on the grass.

Our dessert arrives. My tart is sharp, flaky and delicious. Charles has relented on my waistline. I am allowed chantilly, a little sculptured scoop. His chocolate gateau is awash with real cream. This is a perfect moment. We are rich, happy people, who have already eaten more than is good for us. The appalling children have demanded justice, and justice has been done. Three scoops of ice cream all round at the revolutionary table and all the riots are over. There is a moment of relative calm. All their armaments are laid out on the tablecloth. Amidst the slurps and clatter of contentment we hear Dogwoman disputing her bill.

I peer out into the dim blue gloom. The fisherman is still there. He has set up a stocky triangular rod with an odd metal box at one end. He is attaching a longer piece of metal to the snout. It looks too thick to be an ordinary rod. Perhaps he sets one there for the night and returns in the morning.

'What did you say, Charles?'

Oh God. I have been caught out. Not listening.

But Charles is in his mellow mood. He is beginning to describe his firm's French competitors and the meetings, at which they reveal their volatile Gallic temperaments. And as if to prove his point the children begin shouting again. They have finished their ice cream and they now want to go home. The truly extraordinary thing about this family is their utter lack of awareness that anybody else is present in the restaurant. They assume their right to molest, disturb and destroy without let or hindrance, simply because, in proportion to all the other groups, they are many, we are few. I hear my own voice, like a tap leaking across the years, in full self-righteous, propagandist blast.

'And the heterosexual nuclear families are the most crucial slab in the pattern – a breeding machine to reproduce the labour force and the consumers. That is the place where women and men first learn their roles, how to be serfs and victims, and how to be the masters.'

Kelly grins, a wide clean smile across his young face, which knows too much to be so young.

'You know babe, sometimes I feel I understand the psychos who just climb up to the tops of high buildings and pick off everyone they see.'

Through the blue twilight I hear a faint, decisive click from the other side of the canal. The fisherman is sitting comfortably behind an automatic machine-gun.

He has opened fire.

The first ones to die are the sleek, chic woman and her dog. She has paid her bill and is standing, ready to go, with her little dog tucked beneath her arm. She is caught in the high fire, which shatters the glass in the sliding doors opening onto the terrace. The obsequious maitre d', a nice chap who finished his training in London and had a wonderful time in Wandsworth, is sent spinning round by the force of the bullets. He looks as if he is dancing. The glass splinters into spiders' webs. Shivers of fine glass fall into my apricot tart. The screaming begins as some people inexplicably hurl themselves at the open doors, directly into the line of fire. The children are screaming. Their weapons are useless now. The blonde child has his brains spattered in a satisfying mess all over his plastic ray guns, which leap like popcorn off the table. The fisherman is spoilt for targets as the restaurant surges up in disbelief before flinging themselves to the floor.

Charles has three neat holes evenly spaced across his splendid chest. Takka takka takka as he is flung over backwards, chair and all, with a mighty crash. I have the impression he is steaming. I fling myself ecstatically upon him, as I usually do when we have just had sex, me on top. Somewhere or other I know that I have not been killed yet. But I expect to be at any moment. All the lights have gone out. He has fired at the lights. There is still a light on in the men's lavatory and somebody is crawling towards it. Then he pauses, slumps, twitches, lies still. The noise stops. And all I can hear is the unearthly tinkle of broken crockery. Charles's white shirt is smeared with blood. My face is on his chest. Oh my God, he is still breathing. There is an appalling gurgle in his throat. His blood spreads across my face, into my mouth. It has a strange, distinctive smell. I see that my legs and arms are flooding with blood from a thousand tiny shafts of glass, as if I am a martyred saint, a female St Sebastian.

The most memorable thing about Charles was the way he died. Peacefully, mercifully, in total silence, with a slight burp as he swallowed his own blood. His eyes were wide open in amazement and his raw silk shirt was ruined.

The tie he had purchased in Paris was neatly pierced by a single bullet. Good-oh. I hated that tie, gaudy, yellow and pretentious, with tiny, dark-blue squares, his one mistake.

I hear water running into a basin. I hear someone crying in huge gulps, and beneath that a terrible, absolute silence. Then I hear his footsteps on the terrace. How has he crossed the canal? It is the fisherman, handsome as a freedom fighter in a nationalist liberation struggle, his sniping rifle, *Fusil à Répétition,* F1, the standard service rifle for the French Army, balanced on his hip. He has many guns, all French Army issue. He is like a sculptured monument in praise of a new country, his long hair tied back, his face young, clear, unlined, glittering like an angel.

I see his boots, laced, military, damp grass clinging to the heels. Is he wearing army fatigues? Yes, military green. I shall always remember him. Keep your eyes shut. Not tight. The dead never have to make an effort to stay dead. Don't breathe. Pray that he thinks Charles's blood is yours. Oh my God, our waiter is twitching. Impossible not to tense up at the dull, murky thud of the bullets sinking into nearly dead flesh at point-blank range. I had to talk about that afterwards in interviews. I tried to make it as vivid as possible.

He must have another gun. He has. He is using a silencer. Spectral, authoritative, the angel whom I have involuntarily summoned hovers above me. Then moves on.

4

MOVING

I knew who they were as soon as I heard the address: Ellis Williams and his wife. Her sister lives with them now. They were very religious people, the last of the faithful left praying when the Baptist chapel closed its doors. The old father used to be the minister. My wife tells me that he was famous for his hell-fire sermons. Anyone who went to a rock concert was damned for ever. Ellis Williams had to wait fourteen years before the old man gave him permission to court his younger daughter. She must have been a dutiful child. Any normal woman would have told her father to get stuffed and made a dash for it. That chapel was a bleak place. Mount Zion they called it. And all around there was nothing to see but the blue hills, the upland marshes and the stealthy mist.

My wife was a Baptist. She used to go there in the old days, until her family moved down into town. They're local people. It doesn't matter how long you live here, if you're English, you're an outsider. I went into the family removal business when my father-in-law retired, but I never learned to speak the language properly. My fault really. I've picked up a few words here and there, but it doesn't come naturally. My wife's a native speaker. She always apologizes to me before easing herself back into nattering with her Mam or her friends. I always say, 'Don't mind me, love. Carry on.' It's a little ritual we have. She was brought up never to speak her mother tongue in front of English people, but that seems silly when I'm the only one there. Anyway, she's much more at home speaking her language. It's as if she's snuggling her feet into her slippers and making herself comfortable.

Well, Ellis Williams rang up and told me they had decided to come down the mountain at last. They'd lived there all their lives. And at first it all sounded very sensible. They're all three of them getting on. It's been twelve years since the old hell-fire preacher was called to his immortal reward. His wife had died before him and old Farmer Evans, the elder sister's husband, had put an end to his days with his own shotgun. It was given out as an accident, but I heard otherwise in the local shop. A tragic accident. To spare the family. Ellis Williams and both his sisters were suffering from arthritis and one of them was booked into Bronglais for the hip operation. They were rich people. They owned several properties in town. When the lease fell due on one of the bigger properties, they decided to tidy up the wallpaper and move in themselves. I can't say I blame them. The winters up there are unimaginable. The wind cuts you in half. There are no trees. Just the old house and the chapel surrounded by boggy graves: Mount Zion.

Not that he told me all that. My wife knows all the local gossip. And for some reason she took it up in a big way. She wanted to know exactly what was going on up at Zion. It must have been her memories of the old hell-fire preacher and his threats of burning flames for ever.

People can be very strange. In my business you accept whatever they tell you, no questions asked, and think your own thoughts.

It was a bleak and terrible day when we drove up the mountain to collect Ellis Williams and the sisters. It was like driving back in time. When we left the sea it was sunny, not too warm, but with a fresh wind rifling the gulls. By the time we reached the mountain the rain was actually turning to sleet on the windscreen and there were runnels of water pouring across the road. I could see the chapel from miles away. As we came closer, we noticed that the big windows were shattered, many slates gone from the roof, the plain stone crosses lopsided among the graves. I saw the door swinging in the gale and the rain driving past onto the tiles. The sheep were already there, cowering inside the porch, their backs braced against the wind. Another year and even the roof would be gone.

The house was a long, low stone building once painted white, but now greening with age. There were no animals in the yard, no dogs, no hens. The day was half-dark, but we saw no lights in the house or in any of the sheds. There was a large open-backed truck parked by the abandoned sheep pens and no sign of Ellis Williams' old Land Rover. We climbed out into the drizzle and made for the front door. It swung open and there stood the elder sister, a tiny woman with grey hair, a crooked back and a daemonic stare. Not the sort of woman you'd want to take on in an argument. I began to revise my opinion concerning Evans' suicide. He'd probably opened his mouth once too often and she'd stuck the gun in it.

'Everything is ready,' snapped the widow Evans. She made it clear that she'd already packed the kettle. My boy Gazza stepped back on my toes. The other sister was quieter, trembling, as if she had the beginnings of Parkinson's. We found ourselves looking at a heaped mass of boxes and four stained barren walls.

A lot of clients like to pack themselves. Which is understandable. It's a personal matter, isn't it? But clients who pack are the very devil to load. They never read the booklets I send out with the insurance forms. Giant boxes, full of books, precious crockery in flimsy bags. We sometimes have to repack them on the spot, and that takes time. The family in Zion were exactly like that, an incompetent mess of straw and string.

There were only three cases packed to a professional standard stacked in the shed. Ellis Williams explained that the three long boxes bedded in thick straw and wooden frames – new, specially built – contained precious equipment. He'd be taking them himself, on the truck, but would be glad of a hand loading up. Both sisters came out and stood in the rain to watch us do this. They made Gazza nervous. We sloshed about in the muddy yard, getting cold and soaked. Ellis Williams spent a good hour rigging up a tarpaulin securely over the cases while we hauled all their sagging boxes into the back of my lorry. The rain never ceased. By midday the world was darkening all around us.

'For God's sake,' muttered Gazza, 'let's finish up fast. My feet are soaked and the old woman spooks me.'

It's true that we don't see people at their best.

Ellis Williams would lead the way down the mountain in his hired truck with his precious cases. We could have stuck them in the back of the lorry. We had the space. But he wouldn't hear of it. When I made the suggestion, the older sister pounced. She spoke in her own language, so I didn't understand her. I don't think it would have made much difference if I had.

'*Beth ddwedest ti wrtho fe?*'

'*Dim byd. 'Dyw e' ddim o'i fusnes e'. Mae'n cael ei dalu i symud ein trysor. Does dim rhaid iddo wybod dim byd.*'

The only word I understood was *trysor,* which means 'treasure'. Obviously everything that had been under the floorboards was now in the back of the truck. And that was it. They locked the door of the old house. The key was a nineteenth-century antique, probably the only one in existence.

'When're the new people moving in then?' I asked.

'The new people?'

'Yes.'

'No one is coming here.'

'Oh, I'm sorry. I misunderstood. I thought you'd sold the house.'

'Sold it?' The elder sister gasped. 'We would never sell our home! Never!'

Ellis Williams caught me by the arm as I climbed into the cab.

'Don't mind her. She's upset about the chapel. It's been sold to an architect from Swansea. He's going to do it up as a studio or something. We opposed the sale, of course. But there aren't any of the elders left. It was the grave-yard, you see.' He trailed off.

I said that I quite understood, but they were strange people and I was cold, wet and longing to be gone. Like I say, we don't see people at their best. Moving is right up there alongside bereavement as one of the most stressful events in all our lives. Some people never get over it. These three had lived all their lives on Mount Zion. Isn't it supposed to be the sacred mountain, where Moses saw God? Or is that Sinai? All we saw was mist and sheep as we pulled away from the darkened house in driving rain. The chapel loomed up on our right in the eerie, failing light. Gazza looked at it anxiously, as if we would still hear the voices of the faithful raised in praise of the Lord. But all we heard was the wind soughing through the broken panes and the splintered door banging against the crumbling stone.

★

The long descent was slowed by grey sheets of rain lashing the windscreen. I had the wipers on maximum speed and the headlights on full. But even so we saw very little ahead of us as the lorry lurched round the hairpin bends, following Ellis Williams and his tarpaulin, flapping on the rear of the truck.

I thought that we were over the worst when the accident happened.

I was about fifty yards behind Ellis Williams. There was a sharp bend and the road was awash with water. My brakes held, but I didn't react quickly enough. A Land Rover leaped out of one of the fields to the right. He seemed to think that he owned the road and didn't even look to see if there was anyone coming. I don't think he even knew what he'd hit. He just surged out of the mud with a rush and slammed into the cabin of the truck. I came out of the trees just behind, crashed on my brakes and slithered into the back of Ellis Williams' carefully stacked treasures. Someone's horn was stuck screaming.

Then we all sat there, wedged into one another, lights on, engines running, that horn blaring into the silence. I looked out into the coming dark. The rain now rendered everything barely visible. After what seemed like hours I turned off the engine and climbed stiffly out of the cab. Gazza just sat there, staring. The horn stopped. I heard a dog howling.

'It's shock,' I said to no one in particular. 'I've read about shock.'

The rain drenched my face and ran down my glasses. I'd buckled the back of the truck in front and smashed open the cases. All that careful packing gone for nothing. I remember thinking that if he'd let me load them up in my lorry, they wouldn't have shifted. They'd have been safe. Then I noticed that the case nearest to me contained another antique box, none too clean, which was shattered all down one side. I thought I was hallucinating. Inside the box was a human arm, blackened and hideous, with black rags clinging to it. I stood staring for a moment. Then I climbed up the muddy bank to peer in at the family.

Ellis Williams was slumped on his wife's lap with blood oozing down his face. The windscreen was shattered. The women sat still, gazing out at the rain. I pulled at the door. It was jammed.

'The other side,' I shouted. 'Get out the other side.'

But of course, they couldn't. The bloke who'd rammed them was wedged into their door. So I went round to him.

'Can you back up?' I yelled through the window.

'I've hurt my leg,' he wailed. He was a big man with a red face and very little hair left.

'Yes. But can you back up?'

Well, someone had to take charge. I just kept waving at him until he put the Land Rover into reverse and backed into the other hedge. The wheels spun in the mud. The dog in the back of the Land Rover set up a furious, bellowing roar. I left him shouting at the dog.

Ellis Williams was unconscious. His wife had tried to stop the bleeding, but it's not really possible with head wounds. So we hauled him out onto the wet bank and covered him up as best we could. So far as I could see the sisters were all right. They sat on the bank in the rain, one on either side of him. I turned off the engine. Gazza climbed out and sat down beside them. His hair was plastered to his face in seconds.

'Fucking hell, man,' he muttered. Then he just sat there, staring at Ellis Williams. He didn't even glance into the back of the truck.

I called up the police and the ambulance on the mobile, but by the time they got there, over forty minutes later, no one had moved. The dog had shut up. The chap in the Land Rover was still sitting at the wheel, shaking all over, and the four of us sat on the bank in the rain and cold with Ellis Williams laid out in our midst.

The open coffin, for that's what it was, received the blessing of God's sacrament, the baptism of flood rain, for the first time in many, many years.

★

There had to be an inquest. Ellis Williams was declared dead on arrival at hospital. Rhys Edwards, that was the bloke responsible for the entire fiasco, had a fractured shin bone. But the other two cases had also contained corpses in various stages of decomposition. So there were four people dead at the scene of the crash, but only one of them recently killed.

When we finally got to court the case was heard by the coroner. We all sat together on the front bench: Mrs Evans, Ellis Williams' widow, Gazza in his best suit and me, just as we had sat on the bank in the raining dark. Rhys Edwards sat on another bench with his lawyer. No one was on trial exactly. They were just trying to ascertain the facts. I was first up. I said that I hadn't realized, or even suspected, what was in the cases until the accident. I felt bad about that. It may have been the truth, but it still seemed to me as if I was trying to get out of something. Mrs Evans noticed this. She was a more sensitive woman than I'd imagined. She squeezed my hand when I sat down. I heard her whisper something to her sister.

'A ddylen nhw glywed y gwirionedd?'

'Cymaint o'r gwirionedd ag sydd raid – dim ond Duw sy'n gwybod pob peth.'

But I didn't understand. Only one word: *Duw*. God. Then it was Mrs Williams who stood up.

I wasn't the only one who was taken aback at what happened. You have to understand, she was a tiny, insignificant, grey-haired woman of seventy or more, and when I'd first seen her she'd been trembling, somewhat unstable on her pins. Now she was determined in her step. When she spoke her voice was clear, ringing, sure. And as she raised her face to the court she became younger, luminous.

There had been no questions. No discussion was necessary. The family could not be separated. The chapel was sold; the house was too remote and primitive for them to remain upon the holy mountain. But at least they would all leave together, the three of them and their father, mother and her sister's beloved husband. Until they found their final resting-place within the Everlasting Arms. The Baptist preacher had been an austere, uncompromising man, dedicated to the Lord's Will, but he had also been gentle, tender, a loving husband and devoted father, who adored his daughters and had earned rather than enforced their obedience. In life and in death he remained a faithful servant of the Lord, even as they too strove to be worthy of their place, as God's children.

'We understand little of God's nature, but we know where He is to be found. Zion is not merely a place; it is a way of seeing. And that is the otherworldly treasure we possessed and were bound to preserve and defend.'

And then she spoke of what Zion had meant to her, in her youth, as a young woman, how the beauty of God had touched their lives on that lonely mountain. A remote place? Yes, perhaps, but haunted by presences, charged with God's grandeur, aflame with the glory of His Word. She had seen, with her own eyes, the wind transforming the hands of God into rushing shadows across the hills. She had felt His breath in the mist, heard His voice in the hail and the winter storms. She had seen all the wealth of His Kingdom in the softness of early spring and the dew melting from green graves. They had known in their own flesh what it meant to dwell in the House of the Lord. And yes, she had stayed, because, to her, Mount Zion was the richest place on earth.

The woman stood before the court, transfigured.

'And they shall not hurt nor destroy in all my holy mountain, for the earth shall be full of the knowledge of God, as the waters cover the sea.'

5

THE STRIKE

I was booked on the 2.30 p.m. ferry from Portsmouth to Caen on 1st July. We heard about the strike on the news the day before. The fishermen had blockaded all the Channel ports, including Le Havre, where a P&O ferry was stranded at sea, unable to enter the harbour. The fishermen were demanding a diminution of the petrol tax because the price of fuel was eating up their slender profit margins. The farmers came out in support of the fishermen and blockaded the Channel tunnel. They set fire to hay bales and poured several tons of potatoes over the access roads. We watched the late TV news at 10 p.m. and saw a huge combine harvester straddling the road. There were angry scenes when stranded British holiday-makers trying to get home shrieked abuse at the picket line and the police standing directly in front of them. It looked as if the police were protecting the strikers. Most of the holidaymakers were elderly and rich. They climbed out of their Range Rovers and swore in French. We were very impressed. On the English side of the Channel the motorway was backed up with lorries for over twenty miles. The holidaymakers on our side were families with children under school age. They all pointed out that fuel was much cheaper in France than it was in England, so what could possibly be the matter? We weren't on strike and had more cause to be. My family all agreed. I pointed out that the French are more heavily taxed. They pay taxes that we have never even heard of, like the Allocations Familiales and the Taxe Professionnelle, which you have to pay if you're in work, any kind of work, from literary translation to road repairs. The rise in fuel prices was the last straw.

But the fishermen settled, the blockade was lifted and I sailed away.

I spend the summers in the South of France and try to finish translating at least one book. I like the three months' concentrated work. I like living in the language from which I am translating and I like lying in the sun.

When I am driving I listen to the news. And that was when I realized that something was wrong. The fishermen had indeed settled, but only by agreeing to a reduction in their social security payments. The fuel prices stayed where they were. And this directly hit the lorry drivers who were muttering threats in the wings. They now decided to move centre stage and blockade the petrol depots, refineries and all the ports where crude oil was delivered.

I decided to fill up on the last leg of my journey just in case we were faced with a fuel shortage. My tank was over three-quarters full when I reached the house.

'*Vous avez bien fait,*' said my neighbour, handing me the keys.

I rent a house in a tiny hamlet where there are three other holiday houses and only two resident families. The *boulanger* comes past every day, but there are no shops and no garage. The nearest town is over eight miles away, along a winding precipice. I went in next day to do some panic buying in the supermarket. Other people were doing exactly the same thing. They were already out of fresh milk.

One of my English friends rang up.

'Good thing you got through before the petrol blockade. Some of my relatives are stuck in a campsite on the Loire. The pumps are dry and so is the mobile home. No diesel to be had for love nor money.'

I bought a jerrican from the hardware store and filled that up in the afternoon. I had to hide the car and queue for an hour. No one was allowed to fill up their car *and* a spare can. Then I drove home and settled down on the back terrace to sit it out. My translation rolled off the printer, almost 3,000 words a day for the first few days. It was a gripping psychological thriller about an actress who was convinced that someone was stalking her, but could not identify the man or describe him. I celebrated my rapid progress with a slug of gin at seven o'clock, when I turned off the computer and turned on the television. But the news was not good: the talks between the government and the three main unions representing the lorry drivers broke down after two days. The prime minister made desperate statements about never giving way, which seemed most unwise. I met my neighbours on the bridge.

'*C'est le bras de fer,*' they all nodded, as if it was a known strike ritual which would always end in compromise and agreement.

But it didn't. And events seemed to move with alarming rapidity. By the end of a week the petrol pumps across the country were dry. The government called out the army to raise a military barricade around the fuel distribution centres in the Paris region so that the lorries couldn't capture them and the capital would continue to function. The TV news now dealt with one single topic, as if the rest of the world had ceased to exist.

My translation continued apace. The actress was forced to undergo psychiatric treatment for paranoid delusions.

Meanwhile, the fuel reserves at the airports ran dry and many internal flights were cancelled. The farmers, who were suffering every bit as much as the lorry drivers from the tax on fuel, blockaded the railway tracks, disrupting the TGV. The taxi drivers came out, thousands of them, in support of the lorry drivers, and stifled the Paris ringroads with a slow-moving convoy named *'Opération Escargot'*. This entailed driving round and round the *périphérique* at five kilometres an hour until their petrol ran out, and when it did they built barricades out of the stranded taxis. The remaining petrol stations, which still had reserves, were requisitioned by the state for the emergency services. You had to show your *carte professionnelle* and were rationed to 150 francs' worth of fuel each. No one else got any petrol whatsoever.

The country staggered to a halt.

But what was really extraordinary was that more and more groups joined the strike. The driving schools came out and took over the centre of Toulouse. The shepherds from the Haute-Savoie came down from the mountains with their flocks, protesting at the falling price of lamb and the prevalence of foreign imports. They besieged the Senate, dressed in their traditional broad hats and capes, menacing the police with their crooks, dogs and guns. Then they occupied the Luxembourg Gardens. The sheep ate all the ornamental hedges and the flowers. Nobody felt that the shepherds were going too far. The construction workers drove their huge digging machines and mobile cranes onto the runways and terrorized the airports. Strange professions such as the cultivators of the oyster beds joined the barricades near Sète in the Midi, demanding compensation for a virus that had infected their harvest. The makers of salt around La Baule in Brittany downed tools and scattered mountains of salt on the steps of the Prefecture. The *chasseurs,* objecting to the European regulations limiting the days on which they were allowed to shoot everything that moves, occupied the motorways and all the arterial routes, waving their guns at the last motorists left upon the roads. The motorways linking Spain and Italy across the southern rim of the country were closed by our local *chasseurs,* some of whom I knew. They drove up and down in both directions, many of them packed into single vehicles, patrolling the empty lanes, still wearing their red hats.

The fishermen decided that it was time to demand yet more concessions and blockaded the Channel ports and the tunnel once again. By mid-July a general strike had been declared.

We were also in the midst of a mighty heat wave. I have a theory that industrial discontent prospers in good weather. It takes courage and stamina to gather and demonstrate in rain and snow. It takes real verve to riot. But in that daily veil of heat and the long sweating nights, anything was possible. The strike held.

The heroine of my translation became convinced that she was the victim of uncanny forces and the solitary witness to the progress of something entirely sinister, the harbinger of apocalypse. No one else could see it, but she could. Her psychiatrist concluded that she was mad and should be sectioned. She was locked away in the asylum.

The images on the television grew more and more alarming. The riot police were attacked by striking construction workers when they tried to move the demonstrators off the runways at Roissy. There was a major explosion at one of the storage depots guarded by the army just outside Paris. It was almost certainly a bomb and many people were badly hurt. A huge fire spread to the surrounding warehouses before the army's emergency fire service could spring into action – the *pompiers* were on strike and had been for weeks. Mediterranean forest fires burned out of control in the Var and the Vaucluse. The townspeople of Manosque had to defend their own homes. Part of the town was reduced to ashes. We saw pictures of the *maire,* weeping in his wife's arms. Shops, which had been open in the mornings only, now began to close their doors for ever. There was no one left on the streets. I had only half a tank of petrol left.

Then the *boulanger* ceased to descend the precipice. He was running on his reserves and the trip wasn't worth it for only three houses. Some people lucky enough to be living on the border could still get petrol in Luxembourg. We saw pictures of them filling up their tanks, anxious, but jubilant. Britain, Belgium, Switzerland, Italy and Germany closed their frontiers with France. I was trapped.

At first I wasn't really afraid. I said to myself, this can't go on. They must negotiate. They must be negotiating in secret. But something happened on 20th July, which put the wind up me with a vengeance. One of my neighbours, a nurse named Geneviève who has three small children, knocked upon my door.

'Anybody there? *Est-ce qu'il y a quelqu'un?*'

I was still progressing well with my translation, now a beautifully written evocation of childhood, which my heroine was recounting to her psychiatrist while he drew pictures of palm trees. The translation took my mind off political events, but I started in alarm when I heard my neighbour's voice. I had begun to fear the knock upon the door.

She wouldn't come in.

'We're going north to my family in Vichy,' she said, 'I think we'll be safer in the city. François can't get to work any more anyway. You'll be all right. Nobody comes down this road. And the Chiffres are still there. We'll have to use the last of the petrol to get to Vichy. So we won't come back until the strike is over.'

'When do you think it will end?'

'*Alors . . . ça,*' she shrugged her shoulders. I kissed her goodbye.

The EDF workers came out a day or so later and the lights failed. I could no longer work on the computer. I continued the translation by hand. I had no more hot water in the taps, no more music, no radio and no TV. The telephone still worked. I rang England, but I was unable to say reassuring things to my family.

'It's getting difficult. I've got enough food for weeks, months even. But no more fresh food. The fridge doesn't work any more. And I haven't got enough petrol to get out.'

'Could you get to Spain by crossing the mountains on the tiny roads? There are still planes flying from Barcelona. Not from Madrid any more. Haven't you heard? The strike is spreading.'

They rang again on the following day.

'We've been dreadfully worried. Did you know that eight people have been shot dead in Paris?'

'Nothing like that here.'

But in fact I had no more information as to what was happening in the rest of the country. Apparently the army had now been called in to restore order rather than spend their time standing about outside petrol dumps, having stones and bricks thrown at them. Martial law had been declared and Paris had begun to look like it had done during the Occupation. But still the strike continued to deepen and take root. Looting was wide-spread. Someone else had been shot dead in the night while making off with a television set in the centre of Bordeaux. There was an early evening curfew in all the major cities. My family were distraught. They had rung the British Embassy in Paris, but a skeleton staff were dealing with more pressing emergencies. My village was too remotely hidden to be evacuated. There were early signs that the strike had begun to take hold in Britain and in Germany.

I met Madame Chiffre on the bridge daily and she sold me her own home-made bread and fresh vegetables. The Chiffres were elderly peasants of the old school. They were completely undisturbed by the demise of the modern world. They conducted a more or less autarchic existence anyway. They even had salted meat as if we were still in the Middle Ages.

'We could hold out until December,' declared Madame Chiffre, fearless.

'I hope it won't come to that.'

The phone went dead during the first week of August. The Chiffres had never had one and therefore didn't care. We told ourselves that the *boulanger* would soon return and recount all the events of the strike to us, inform us as to what was happening and what we would be well advised to do, as he had done at the beginning. But he never came back. We had no more news of the outside world.

The Chiffres showed me how to heat water. We put a row of buckets out in the sun first thing in the morning and by late afternoon they were boiling. I took modest hot showers in the garden surrounded by string beans, aubergines and dahlias, all shoulder high. The water was then recycled as it flowed into a series of dirt channels, which passed through the vegetables. I continued the translation for an hour or two every day using pen and paper, but I began to spend my time outside, gardening. The translation had in any case become slightly preposterous, for the heroine now believed that she could see God's hand in everything. The story was written from her point of view, but I began to sympathize with the sceptical psychiatrist. The tale had lost all its urgency. As the heroine screeched her improbable prophecies of doom, I passed the days planting lettuces, harvesting aubergines, putting up fences around the vines to keep out the wild boar and killing slugs. We grew courgettes, cucumbers, tomatoes, artichokes, green beans, onions, pumpkins, peppers. I became sunburnt, healthy, and since we had no more news of what was happening outside, peculiarly relaxed and content.

I had moments of doubt. Were we being prudent, holed up here in a green ravine, locked away from the world?

'*Ecoutez-moi bien*,' said Monsieur Chiffre, 'the First World War didn't pass by here and neither did the Second. If there's a war, it won't affect us. All we have to do is wait.'

So that was all we did. And we lived as people in that village had always done. I washed my clothes in the *lavabo*. It was a very soothing activity. The stream had been diverted directly into the old stone washhouse. There was a basin for soapy clothes and a fresh-water vat for rinsing. The water was bitter and cold, rising from the depths of the mountain. It smelt of thyme and lavender. The Chiffres sold me some soap. No matter how desperate the external situation had become, the economic nexus between foreigner and peasant remained stable. They offered me their goods; I paid cash.

I went to bed at sundown and got up with the fowls to save candles. But I began to notice that the days were getting shorter and the nights slightly colder when I closed the shutters. My watch still worked. It was almost the end of August.

The Chiffres did what they had always done at the year's change. At the end of August they cut the wood for next year. And so we all trooped up the hillside, pulling the barrows behind us. But we no longer used the chainsaw, which was diesel-powered. We sharpened the axe.

Then, one day in September, as I came down to the bridge in the early morning, carrying my washing, I noticed that Madame Chiffre was no longer there. I searched for her beautiful lined face and black headscarf among the bean frames and aubergines. I called out. But I heard only the wind, sighing in the green scrub oaks. Suddenly terrified, I rushed to their house, which was the first one in the village. The shutters were open as they got up earlier than I did, and so was their front door. I knocked and called, but there was no reply. I touched the coffee pot. The fire had died down, but both the range and the cream coffee pot were still warm. As I stepped out of the house I saw that their coats, usually left hanging in the porch, had vanished. Their old van with its tiny reserve of petrol was still there in the garage. It was as if something had swept them away before they had had time to lock the door. I wandered up the road and looked back down at the abandoned village. Then I saw what must have happened. The Chiffres' house was the first one at the village entrance, perched above the neatly weeded allotments. My house and the other three houses were all locked and shut. The Chiffres had appeared to be the only people left in the village, and so they had been taken away. They had not betrayed me.

I sat on the back terrace outside my shuttered house and cried for an hour. Then I pulled myself together and put the buckets out as usual.

While Monsieur and Madame Chiffre were still there it was easy to rationalize our deliberate inaction, our waiting game. We waited; someone would eventually come and tell us it was over. But now that I was alone the silence of the crouching mountains pressed in upon me. I locked up the Chiffres' house carefully and hid the key in the garage. I let the chickens out at dawn, just as Madame Chiffre had always done, and shut them up at dusk. I cared for the gardens. The weather became heavy and oppressive. I waited for the storm to break.

One afternoon the sky darkened. I watched the coming storm through a crack in my shutters. The hens cackled in the shed as the sky cracked apart and the thunder flung itself against the mountains. When the rain eased I walked down to the allotments. And for the first time I noticed the weeds growing in the centre of the roadway. The cars no longer passed; the hunt no longer visited us at the weekends. The dogs had been taken to Vichy with the family of whom we had heard no more. I was alone with the hens and the mountains.

I took my courage in both hands and pumped up the tyres on the bicycle. I calculated that it would take me two hours to cycle into town by the rough back tracks. It was too risky to take the direct route by the main road. I was unable to decipher what it was that I feared. A mass of enraged strikers? A line of tanks? A hungry horde of starving peasants? None of this was likely. But until I knew what had happened to the Chiffres I preferred to pass unseen through the damp bush. The dirt road was uneven and overgrown, but the crushed plants beneath my wheels smelt bitter and sharp. Two rabbits shot across my path, startled. No one had passed over the mountains for months. I noticed that the birds were bolder; they waited, intently watching my approach before crashing away through the undergrowth. Buzzards circled casually overhead; they too were watching. My presence was unusual rather than frightening. It was as if we no longer had dominion over the creatures of the earth. Nothing fled before me any more.

The electric cables and the phone lines were apparently intact. I stopped on the bluff above Belleraze to catch my breath and looked across into the village. I heard nothing but the wind. The houses were locked and shuttered and all the vehicles had disappeared. Yet still I felt puzzled rather than afraid.

The last bit of my journey was downhill. I could have ridden fast. The road was asphalted but overgrown. I pushed the bike cautiously, stopping often to listen. But I heard and saw nothing. The Church of Notre Dame de Nazareth was locked, but it was always locked, even before the strike, so there was nothing unusual on the outskirts of town. What was odd was the silence. It was hot and windy. I was fiercely aware of the rustling oak and the whistle of the pines. But I could hear nothing else. The church clock had stopped. I waited for the quarter hour to chime, but heard nothing. There were no passing cars, no dogs barking, no voices. At this time of year, mid-September, the *vendange* should have been underway. There should have been dozens of people bearing huge plastic baskets, combing the vineyards, advancing steadily down the rows of vines in ragged lines, laughing and arguing. There should have been tiny tractors hauling narrow red trailers behind them at the edges of the long green rows. I saw the grapes rotting on the stems, covered in wasps and flies.

I hid the bike in a dry culvert and crept close to the garden walls overlooking the gully. But when I peered over the walls I saw no one. There were abandoned plastic toys lying on browned lawns in the gardens. Geraniums had shrivelled and died in their pots, a shutter banged in the gust. Some of the houses stood open, as if their owners had just stepped out to get the bread. I could see the vivid plastic pattern of a tablecloth skewed sideways on a bench in one of the kitchens. I did not knock. I did not call. I sensed at once that the houses were empty and that there was no one there.

But despite the emptiness I did not feel safe. I looked carefully at the disintegrating roadway. There were deep, even slices creating a rutted, broken surface in the melted asphalt and on the gravel drives. These were the tracks of tanks, still visible but fading fast. The ruts were filling up with weeds and dust. If a tank had passed that way it was long ago. Keeping close to the walls, I advanced down the medieval streets towards the *route nationale*. Just to the left was my garage, which had been requisitioned for the emergency services, over two months ago. I saw the ELF sign and the elevated petrol prices still glaring offensively above the forecourt. The revolving placard ELF/OUVERT rattled round and round in the wind. This was where it had begun, with the transporters' strike and the fuel blockade. And so this was the place to search. I listened. The rhythmic rattling was unnaturally loud. I could hear nothing on the road. No cars, no tanks, no voices.

The dustbins lay empty and overturned in the alleyway. One or two plastic bags flapped against the signposts. I righted one of the green plastic dustbins and quietly climbed aboard. I then had a clear view of the petrol station. At first I saw nothing unusual. The station was deserted. One window was smashed and the glass lay in ugly shattered piles over the steps. The wind carried odd sheets of newspaper round the forecourt, pulling them into the air, then letting them fall. The water buckets had been overturned. But the odd creaks and thumps did not cover the deeper silence, the cavernous emptiness.

Then I saw something.

Beneath the wall, quite close to me in fact, next to the diesel pump, lay the body of a man. He was still wearing his gendarme's uniform. His hair ruffled slightly in the windy sunshine; a pool of brown, caked liquid surrounded his chest and the upper part of his body. I stared and stared, transfixed with shock. It was not the horror of seeing somebody who was clearly dead, which I had never seen before, but of seeing anybody at all. Why had this body been left behind? I leaned forward. The face was turned away from me. I heard a gentle buzzing. Suddenly I realized that the eyes and cheek were black with flies.

I leaped down from the dustbin and ran. The bicycle was forgotten. It was, in any case, useless if I could no longer travel on the roads. I chose the short cut back over the mountains to my village. On the trails in the wilderness I was no longer cautious. I simply wanted to get home to the small place that had seemed so safe. I checked the house carefully to see if anyone had entered the buildings in my absence. But everything was exactly as it had been at my departure. I shut up the protesting hens, closed all the shutters and locked all the doors. I never opened the shutters again and for days after my expedition to the town I lived in an uncanny half dark, paralysed with dread.

But the weather began to change. We had days of stormy rain and I was reduced to watching the fire or watching the road. The gardens died back. I was living out of tins and the conserves sealed with liquid paraffin. I still had enough food to hold out for months and an ample supply of candles. I hated washing in cold water, but found another method of heating huge quantities. The giant hooks in the chimney were left over from daily life in the 1800s. I suspended a grim black pot stolen from the Chiffres' household over my open fire, and in my heart I blessed the rich Parisians who had restored the house, keeping all the original features. I now wore multiple layers of clothes against the morning cold, battened down the hatches and prepared to withstand the siege, the long wait.

I abandoned the translation. If the days were sunny I sat, hidden in the grass, watching the hens scratching by the river. I had not heard the sound of my own voice for over six weeks. I wanted, more than anything else, to go home. According to my watch it was October 23rd. Early on the next day I packed a small rucksack with what now appeared to be the only essential things, warm clothes, dried fruits, sausage. I pushed away the rest, my books, the abandoned translation, the useless computer, my city shoes. I didn't even include a comb. I had been steadily reducing myself to two needs: food, heat. I had passed beyond everything else.

My plan, in so far as I had one, was to get to Narbonne, and from there to steal a boat that could take me to Spain. I even imagined being able to row down the coast. The weather had settled again into warm autumn days with the chill coming in the mist at night. I let the chickens out for the last time and set off into the *garrigue*. Once again I avoided the roads. But I saw no one. I passed a burnt-out shed in which the farm machines still stood like Jurassic monsters, attenuated, blackened. Everywhere across the plateau of the Minervois I saw grapes rotting on the vine. Some of the vineyards had been horribly trampled by the wild boar, which now occupied the land. I lay down in the shade of a wall and slept for an hour, awakening only when the sun shifted and touched my forehead. By midday I came within sight of the motorway.

I realized that the major axes across France might still be open and patrolled, but I had to cross the motorway to get to the sea. I approached the shale embankment, keeping low, staying out of sight. I lay flat on my stomach, turned my ear to the ground and listened. I could hear nothing but the wind. Had the vibrations of vehicles been close I would have heard them. But there was nothing, nothing. I raised myself onto my hands and knees and peered through the metal crash barrier. There was grass growing in the cracks on the motorway, sand blown into patterns by the wind, bundles of dried gorse uprooted by the storms, now browned and discarded in the last sun of the dying season. I took a deep breath and stood up.

★

As far as I can see in both directions, towards Béziers and Perpignan, there is nothing, nothing but light, grass, sand, wind. Before me lies the city of Narbonne. The suburban gardens are dried up and overgrown. There is washing still hanging on the line in one of the paved yards, visible from the road. The gates to the *pépinières* are firmly locked and chained. I peep through the wire. A row of concrete Venus statuettes, diminishing in size, pose on the other side of a brackish pond in which foaming waste floats on the surface. The fountains have long since ceased to bubble. The traffic lights are blank. A burned-out car rests on its side in the corner of the roundabout. The sand has blown against the remaining seats and metal struts, building up into undulating piles. It has lain like that for weeks, maybe months, untouched.

I become bolder and move out from the shadow of the walls. I step onto the abandoned roadway and walk straight into the deserted, silent city. There is old rubbish tipped across the streets and I see two cats, the first I have seen anywhere, scavenging in the piles. The door of a house is left ajar. There are still plates and a bottle of olive oil abandoned on the table, as if the people had been about to eat and were then swept away. I notice a row of candles on the dresser and conclude that the family had still been there when the electricity died around us. But that had been over eight weeks ago. I pass smashed and looted shops. A huge poster offering me unlimited Internet access if I sign up with *wanadoo.fr* leers out in tatters from the electrical wholesalers. Some of the demonstration models are still intact, wired up, chained down, the screens black and silent for evermore. Some shops are neatly locked, with the green mesh or opaque steel grilles in place. Cars lie abandoned everywhere. I skulk through the side streets, hoping to see another human being, alive or dead.

But there is no one beneath the trees on the boulevard by the canal, no one in the main square, gazing down at the excavated Roman road, all that remains of the lost empire. There is no one in the restaurants, no one on the terraces, where the café tables and chairs lie flung in random piles among the rubbish and the overturned municipal dustbins.

I enter the cloisters of the cathedral and at once I sense the change. In all this windy emptiness another human being is a wonderful and terrifying thing. He is there, crouching in the stone shadow of the graves. The priest sits silent in scuffed dark robes. He is perched upon the tomb of an antique archbishop. He is looking at me carefully, but he makes no move, no sign. I stretch out my hands very slowly towards him to prove that I am unarmed. Still, he does not move. I draw closer, walking on tiptoe so that my steps do not echo on the stone. I approach the silent, unmoving priest. For a long moment we stare at one another. I see my own image in his face: dirty, unkempt, savage. But his eyes are burning. When I speak my voice is choked and cracked.

'Is there anybody left here?' This comes out as a whispered hiss.

'Dans la ville de Narbonne? Non. Je ne crois pas.' His voice is steadier than mine, his accent local, his tone matter of fact.

'Where have they gone?'

The priest shrugs his shoulders, indifferent.

'No man knoweth the hour. I wait. As you have done.'

'But what has happened?'

'Vous n'êtes pas au courant? Don't you know? Where have you been, *ma fille?* There's been a strike. *Il y a eu une grève.'*

6

PARIS

The car was a black Mercedes with a 75 registration. That means they come from Paris. We watched it coming down the steep curves towards the village. How many are there? Two people, both wearing dark glasses. They must have rented the Barthez house. He always does summer lets to Parisians. Bit early for the holidays, isn't it? Perhaps they don't have children. Does Monsieur Barthez advertise? Yes, in *Le Monde,* the holiday supplement. And he's got the house with an agency. Must cost a fortune. The agency takes a commission. Worth it, though. He charges more than Mimi does for her little place with the balcony. No comparison, is there? Emile Barthez has got that swimming pool. No water in it, though? Or has he filled it up? Of course he's filled it up. His nephew was down there yesterday. Topping up the chlorine.

'I prefer the sea myself,' says Olivier.

Here's a point of contention. The Barthez family owns the only swimming pool in the village and he has never offered us the use of it, even when the house is empty, not even for a moderate fee. The swimming pool is reserved for the Parisians. So we had better prefer the sea. We haven't any choice.

We stroll down to the bridge and lean pictur-esquely against the stone barriers. We are the reception committee. And we want to get a good look at the Parisians.

They drive into the village very slowly, taking the bend in front of Simone's bungalow with exaggerated care. Pause by the *mairie,* now deserted, unused, the shutters grey as driftwood, banging against the walls in the high winds. Left turn into the main street, leaving the vegetable rows behind them. Beans, cabbages, peas, aubergines, chillies, peppers, courgettes, pumpkins. I've already dug up all the potatoes. One of the cats scuttles out of the path of the oncoming Mercedes. They sweep past. We peer in, stony-faced. Olivier nods his *bonjour.* Well? Hmm. What do we think?

They look as if they have already been on holiday. Both of them are nicely browned. A man and a woman. Young, unsmiling, no children. They pull up in front of the Barthez household, climb out of the Mercedes and begin fiddling with the lock on the storm door. We watch the woman leaving him to get on with it. She turns her attention to the geranium pots that descend the steps. She snaps off the dead flowers with surgical accuracy. She is wearing rings and bracelets made of gold. They are rich, rich, rich. Just like every other holidaymaker who ever comes from Paris.

For most of us, the nearest we get to Paris is our ritual espionage upon the visiting *vacanciers.* Some of us have never been to Paris. Ever. The city remains a symbol in our school books, an image on the television, the source of news and evil things, VAT forms, tax increases and, for me, the closest consulate.

Our village is very isolated. We are eight miles from the nearest post office, thirty miles from the nearest supermarket. The *boulanger* negotiates the tiny climbing roads every day. We can always see him coming. There is one road in and one road out. We are surrounded by mountains covered in scrub oak, the scented *garrigue* and an exploding population of wild boar. We can hear them scrabbling in the river at night. We wring our hands and shake our heads over the damage they do in the vine-yards. Then, as soon as August comes round, we hunt them down and shoot them.

Everyone, except me, lives for the hunt. My nearest neighbour is Papi, well into his eighties and suffering from cataracts, but still roaming the mountainsides, armed to the teeth. The women don't actually go out shooting of course. They stand on the bridge counting the mass of white vans that depart for the wilderness. Then they count the number of wild boar that come back and are laid out in the middle of the village square. They either consign the meat to freezer boxes or turn it into huge steaming pots of herbal deliciousness in a rich red-wine sauce. We shoot to kill. We shoot for the pot. We are hunters. The real thing, undreamed of throughout all the effeminate streets of Paris.

Sébastien is telling me that you have to pay 570 francs to get there and back on the TGV, change at Montpellier. And you had better book weeks in advance: *réservation obligatoire*. But I don't want to go to Paris. I hate going to Paris. I spend too much money and smoke too many cigarettes. I buy too many books and I come home with a hangover.

Simone sits next to me on the green bench. She thinks that Paris was once a beautiful city full of *haute couture* and elegant *soirées,* but that it has now gone to the damnation bow-wows and is full of blacks *sans-papiers,* living in churches or on hunger strike, chained to railings in public places. Once upon a time we earned fair wages if we worked hard, but now there are dozens of young people who don't want to work, and evil bosses running sweat shops, who pay two francs an hour. As if it wasn't hard enough to make ends meet down here, let alone trying to live in Paris.

Olivier, aged eighteen, has just been to Paris with his mates for a dirty weekend and they had never been before. So they spent all their money in Crazy Horse on the Champs Elysées and it was just like it was on TV with geometrically identical girls, bobbed wigs, oval bums and perfect boobs. They all weigh 55 kilos and no more. You daren't put on a sliver of fat. For if you do, you're sacked.

I reflect upon my oozing, lavish rolls of flesh. Then I tell Olivier that I weigh nearly 85 kilos.

'You couldn't get a job at Crazy Horse,' he nods sagely, with all the certainty of youth, 'but even if you lost weight you couldn't anyway. You're too old.'

I have become one of my own worst nightmares, an ageing expatriate with a red nose and a spreading girth who wastes time in bars and sits on a decrepit green bench in the village square, gossiping with whoever else happens to be there. All that I can say in my favour is that I left England because I hated it and that I live in the Midi because the consumptive English, who came here to slide down the bottle and then fill the graveyards, will testify that this is the closest to paradise most of us will ever get. The Americans all agree to that too, each and every one. Mind you, I don't live on the Riviera. That's now full of hamburger bars, tacky film-stars, the Aga Khan's yachts, drug freaks and the massed tramps, fluent at begging in several languages. No, I live in a little bit of France that has a bloody history of Catholic slaughter and a perpetual present of sunshine and vineyards: Cathar Country.

There are twenty-six of us in my village. I'm the only foreigner. Everybody else owns their own land or works in the vineyards, or both. I have a job in the city, a much-envied, much-discussed job, which pays well. I am the English Language schools broadcaster for the entire region. I do three one-hour schools broadcasts every week in term and five specialized professional lessons – eighteen minutes each – with added action dialogue, which go out at 11 p.m. every night during the vacations. I research these carefully and we tape them all beforehand. If you want to get the best out of these courses you have to buy the booklets I've produced. We make a packet out of the booklets.

The live broadcasts are alarmingly stressful. A good deal can go wrong and often does. I'm told by the teachers who either record them or use them directly in their classes, that the live broadcasts make for electrifying listening. The most dreadful being one of our outside events, when I had the bright idea of interviewing English holidaymakers on the beach at Carnon. They had all come down from Luton in a coach and appeared to be taking time off before destroying a dozen bars in the evening. The first sunbathing cadaver looked very promising: huge pink hairy stomach, grimy white handkerchief knotted at the corners, protecting six blonde hairs and a mass of red freckles.

'Excuse me, sir, we are from Radio Cathar. Are you enjoying your holiday?'

'Fuck off, mate!' he roared amiably, and I found myself rowing backwards into a sea of umbrellas.

Well, that's what I do for a living. Needless to say, I have never worked in Paris.

★

Next morning we were all gathered round the *boulanger*'s van, gossiping. Nobody was prepared to admit the fact, but we were waiting for the Parisians. Here they come, in tracksuits, ready to go jogging. In this heat? Goodness, she is very pretty, long black hair, tied back, and a light green sweatshirt which glows against her olive skin. They are both still wearing their dark glasses, the sort that curve around your eyes, like ski-goggles. They are as elegant as successful gangsters.

'*Bonjour.*'
'*Bonjour.*'
'*Bonjour, madame.*'

'*Quatre francs soixante.*'

'*Merci, madame.*'

She speaks.

He says nothing. They both smile, but ever so slightly.

They jog away. She wields her baguette like a sten gun. She has a quite beautiful figure. We are all very impressed.

'Well?'

'*Pas grand chose.*'

We have failed to gather any concrete information. Let's go back and have another look at the Mercedes.

A black Mercedes now bears mythic meanings. We peer in, leaving breath marks on the darkened windows. We want to see the smooth upholstery, the central panel that will glow red at night, the mobile phone in a little leather holster, the carpeted floor, the lack of crisp packets or maps. What we see most clearly are our own faces, reflecting back our grimaces of curiosity.

'It's like the one she died in. A year ago.'

'I was there,' breathes Claudia and we all sit up straight, astounded. 'Yes, I was. A week later. I was in Paris for the day on a coach tour with my grandmother. I was staying with my cousins in Auxerre and I'd never been to Paris, so we went. And the coach driver took us past the Pont de l'Alma where there were flowers on the grass by the golden flame and we even went through the tunnel. And the coach driver went really slowly and pointed out the pillar where the black Mercedes crashed and she died. Just at the moment when she had found love and true happiness.'

'You're making it up,' snapped Olivier.

'No. She did go up to Auxerre. Last September. One week. Don't you remember?' Simone intervenes.

Simone is Claudia's aunt. This is a family quarrel. All the quarrels in our village are family quarrels. Apart from myself, we are all related. Claudia flounces off. Her veracity has been challenged. Olivier is not convinced.

'I don't believe she ever went to Paris.'

But now we are contemplating the events of a year ago and all the intimate geographies of Paris. Would they have crossed the river? Wouldn't have to if they were coming from the Ritz. Where is the Ritz? Isn't it in the Place de la Concorde? No, that's the Hotel Crillon. It's in the Place des Vosges. Has anyone got a map of Paris?

We spy into the interior of the Mercedes. The glove compartment is clearly shut, probably locked. The red eye of their alarm winks back at us. The Parisians have no visible map of their city.

Next day, I do the schools broadcast dictation. This is the last one before *les grandes vacances.*

There are holidaymakers visiting our village.

They have rented a house with a swimming pool.

They drive a big, black Mercedes.

They come from Paris.

They keep fit – cycling, swimming, jogging.

They don't like sunbathing and they eat very late at night.

They continue to behave as if they were in Paris.

★

The green bench in the square sags under the weight of our communal speculation. We hear, but cannot see them using the pool. There are no jolly shouts or sounds of sexy teasing. No giggles, denials, threats, such as usually rise up from holiday swimming pools. We hear an almost simultaneous crash as they hit the water, twice a day with uncanny regularity, very early in the morning and just after six o'clock, when the sun begins to move down the mountain. Every morning and every evening they traverse the chlorinated blue water with steady strokes for half an hour before re-emerging in black tracksuits to vanish up the valley at a steady trot.

It is as if they are in training, not on holiday.

It must be very expensive to train at a gym in Paris. Maybe that's why they come here.

'I went to Paris once,' says Simone, 'just before Christmas. With my sister. The one who lives at Auxerre. We went Christmas shopping at the Samaritaine. And they were selling mistletoe for thirteen francs a bunch outside in the street.'

All eyes swivel down the green bench towards her. Mistletoe is easy to procure from the cousin's orchard in Auxerre. We could go in my car. It may be decrepit, but it'll hold all five of us. We could spend a day doing up little bunches with red ribbons. We could sell them all at ten francs a shot, undercut the competition and spend the rest in Paris. We begin to plan our weekend in the glittering winter city, financed by poison kisses of mistletoe and red ribbons.

In the first week of August the Parisians hire two lightweight racing bikes and reinvent themselves as a lycra-clad speed team. He has one of those watches that measure your heart rate and beep if you slow down. We watch them racing along the edges of the precipice. They continue to say *bonjour* once a day, when they collect their bread. No one has ever heard them say anything else. They have not been seen in St Chinian. Do they ever shop in St Pons? We ask casually in the Ecomarché whether anyone has ever seen the black Mercedes with the Paris registration. No one ever has.

I ring up Emile Barthez to borrow an electric pump, and in the course of idle conversation enquire about the Parisians who are sleeping in his bed and churning up the chemicals in his swimming pool.

'Oh,' he says, surprised, 'what are they like? I don't even know their names. They came through the Holiday Houses agency in Paris.'

'You know,' Simone remarks, 'there's something very odd about that couple from Paris. They never use the barbecue and they never eat outside.'

We all agree. Yes. Odd. No barbecue. Sinister.

★

As the schools broadcasts are finished until *La Rentrée* I am occupied with a new series of *Professional English for Professionals.* We have had a request from the head office of the Gendarmerie in Montpellier. Will we do a mini-series on English for the police? To run during *les vacances*? Of course, says my producer. Delighted. I cannot see why the French police need English. But my producer is adamant.

'It's the only language offered by some international criminals,' she insists. 'Here's our chance to provide a real public service. Not just Computer English, Hotel English, Café English, Tourist Office English, How-to-Book-Your-Flight English, Arriving-in-London English, Doing-an-Arms-Deal English, Eating-Out English, Car-Hire English.'

'OK, OK, I get your point.'

I begin to imagine interrogations in translation. Techniques of subtle menace. It all comes out in Film English. 'Sign this confession you slimy little bastard, or I'll spatter your intestines all over the table.' Which no one ever actually says. What are the most common French crimes? Burglary, theft, assault and doing drugs. Drugs English defeats me. It has never been researched, fashions change daily, and there are no available booklets. I go for Car-Theft English. Now this has actually happened to me in France and I know all the linguistic moves.

My Black Mercedes has been stolen.

Are you quite certain that it has been stolen?

Please write down the registration number.

Was it equipped with an alarm?

Did you leave the vehicle unlocked?

No, the alarm is connected to a central-locking system.

Did it have an Identicar Security number?
Are you on holiday in the area?
Yes, we have rented a house in the mountains.
We are on holiday.
We live in Paris.

★

Their holidays are endless. By the second week in August we decide that they are in fact Olympic athletes in early training for the millennium games. Nothing else explains their relentless, energetic pursuit of cycling, swimming, jogging, gymnastic aerobics and early nights. They go on saying *bonjour* once a day and nothing else. They never take off their dark glasses. They have perfect figures. They are ravishingly beautiful. We have never seen their eyes.

The weather suddenly changes gear, just before *l'ouverture de la chasse*. A white cowl of heat descends like a mask over the village. I go in to work twice a week, cursing, and make scenes at my producer and the technicians. Otherwise I lie in darkened rooms with the windows shut, breathing heavily. We meet on the green bench after eleven o'clock at night to exchange clichés about the *canicule*: worse than last year, quite unbearable, global warming, stream drying up, dogs can't bear it, when will it end? The Parisians set off for their daily run at dawn, before the white cowl drapes the mountains. The thermometer races past 38°C. We water our vegetables twice a day and welcome the *Pompiers-Forestiers,* who turn up in their yellow emergency trucks, gasping for cold water. They are fire watching from the hilltops. They have nothing to report.

★

La chasse est ouverte! Open season. The men dress up in their paramilitary fatigues, topped off by their red caps, and set out for the *garrigue* in their white vans, the dogs howling for joy in the back.

Madame Rubio tells me that she loathes the hunt. Her favourite dog was gored by a wounded boar and cost 750 francs in veterinary repairs. She snorts with irritation as the vans roll past. Yvette is terrified of meeting a wild boar while she is pruning her vines on the red slopes. She hopes that the men will kill them all. I hear the boar, snuffling among my blackberries. I lock all the doors.

And I see them sometimes at night, ponderous, hairy, unhurried, grey in my headlights as I cruise slowly across the mountains, coming home.

The men only hunt in the early mornings. By eleven thirty they are back in the village, sharing the kill, feeding the dogs, sharpening their long, curved knives on the whirling whetstones. The heat is too fierce to go out in the afternoons. The dogs lose the scent and cannot track the boar through the bush. In the afternoons they lie flat, bored by flies, their bells clinking on the shaded gravel.

Papi collars me as I languish on the green bench.

'It's about time you came out hunting with me. You should see what it's all about.'

Papi is eighty-three. He has been threatening to take me out with him on one of these wildlife dawn raids for the past seven years. Suddenly he insists. I understand why: Papi fears that his hunting days will soon be over. And alas, he wants to prove something. He has spent one month this year in the clinic down in Perpignan, dealing with his bronchitis. He's right. I should go. I agree. We stagger back to his house and Papi pours a deadly glass of home-made *eau de vie*, seventy-five per cent pure alcohol. Men sell not such in any shop. Chin, chin, Papi. This is it. We smile at each other beneath the gloom of a forty-watt bulb, all that he will consent to install over his dining-room table, and he takes his gun down from the wall above the fireplace.

We decide to move at dawn on Wednesday next.

But on Tuesday night the police stop me at the motorway exit. Béziers West. They are waving on the other cars. They are looking for someone. My God, they are looking for me. I've been caught in a radar trap. I sit panic-stricken and surrounded. Am I drunk? No, not yet. It's too early in the evening. My tax disc and insurance are in order, but both back tyres are practically bald. And I should have put the thing through the government test over two months ago. I thought I wouldn't go until I had changed the tyres. If they throw the book at me this could mean nearly 5,000 francs' worth of fine. Far more than the tyres and the test put together would ever cost. Shit, shit, shit, shit, fuck, fuck, fuck, fuck, bugger, bugger, bugger, bugger.

'*Vos papiers, Monsieur.*' Pause. '*Excusez-moi. Madame.*'
Madame? Who cares? Go on. Fine me.

'Où habitez-vous?'

You've got the address in front of you, mate. Right there, on my *carte grise.*

He stands there, looking at my papers, *carte de séjour,* passport, credit cards, insurance documents.

'Cest vous qui faites les émissions en anglais pour Radio Cathar?'

'Yes, yes, that's me. Fame at last! Do you listen regularly? To the police broadcasts? Really? And do you find them helpful? Ah yes, that's me. An essential public service. Delighted to be of assistance. *Vive l'entente cordiale.'* Now let me off, Monsieur le Gendarme. I'll change my tyres at once, if not sooner. Only please, please, please, let me go.

Oh dear God, he wants to chat. And to practise his English.

'We very much enjoy your broadcasts. Very interesting. And do you use your own experiences?'

Always. All the time. Drawn from life. Every single sentence. Am I being let off this time? Just this once?

'Do you often talk about people in your village?'

Yes, of course. Not directly. But I like authenticity. All the details about the tramp who burgled Simone's bungalow and ate a tin of peas are just as they happened. It's more authentic. More convincing. May I go?

'And that story about the stolen Black Mercedes?'

Ah yes, good, wasn't it? The Parisians who are on holiday in our village have a black Mercedes. But of course it isn't stolen. I beg you. Let me go.

He waves me on.

173

By the time I get home my encounter with the police has become a Bruce Willis style car chase with crashed barriers, screaming wheels, fast talking and bold lies. Everyone on the green bench is thrilled. We all love a good story.

★

Papi hauls me out of bed at dawn and I stumble after him and his straining dogs. It is beautiful out in the valley, waiting among the vines in the still blue light. We are not far from the village. I can just see the tiled roofs.

The ground is hard and dry. We stumble over the rough white stones in the vineyards. I watch the day hardening, gaining ground. We can hear the bells on the dogs' collars, far away. Papi has an elderly pair of binoculars. Through the smeared lens I can see the red caps of our neighbours; they are perched on the edge of the steep road leading up to Vialanove. We wave from time to time. The breaking day is peaceful and quiet. We are not allowed to start shooting until it is quite light; otherwise we end up killing each other. Suddenly we hear the sound of the dogs, a deep howl, in chorus, lengthening. They have caught the scent. We strain forwards. Yes, I can hear it, far below in the river bottoms, something heavy, rising through the bush towards us. Papi scampers down the vine rows, heading for the road, wielding his gun, nimble and expectant. I watch the freckled hands tightening on the buckles of his sack. You are not allowed to stand around with a loaded gun. If you are going to fire you must charge it up just beforehand. Papi is loading his gun. I stand well back, completely panicked, covering my ears. Oh no! The crashing, howling bush is coming upwards, closer and closer. We are on the road. Papi has levelled the gun, snug against his shoulder. His hands are steady and firm. He knows the boar will cross the road.

The events of the next few moments pass so suddenly before me that I can make no sense of them. There is Papi, standing on the road, ready to shoot. I hear more than one car coming down the curving precipices behind me. And round the corner, surging upwards, heads down, thighs braced, moving at speed, come the Parisians, hurtling straight towards us on their racing bikes, their dark glasses clamped to their faces like black diving goggles, their mouths open. They see Papi pointing his gun directly at them. Shrieking with fear and fury, they skid past us. I cannot understand a word they say, for as they clip me with their elbows, the boar breaks cover with the dogs at his heels and flings himself across the road. Papi fires twice and we are both covered in a great fountain of warm blood as the boar falters, staggers, buckles, falls. We hear the Parisians still screaming; they have almost turned the corner behind us. I am screaming too.

I am overcome with horror. I have never been afraid of the wild boar roaming the hills. Now I see that I should have been. The thing is enormous, with giant yellow tusks. I will never go walking in the mountains ever again. Papi is looking at the boar and at the blood pumping onto the road. He must have shot the monster through the heart. The dogs are swirling around him, slavering, yelping, sniffing at the blood.

Then the police are upon us, all around us, snatching Papi's rifle and raving. A pair of eyes in a face masked by a cagoul is glaring into my face and the muffled mouth is uttering a sequence of unintelligible yells.

I turn around.

There are police everywhere, dressed in dark blue with hoods across their faces, as if they were storming a hijacked plane. I find myself wondering if Papi and I are, in fact, on television. Then I see that there are bodies on the road behind us, all mixed up with racing bikes. And I am screaming,

'Vous avez tué les Parisiens!'

'Shut up,' snaps one of the hooded assassins.

'Go home, Grandad,' he roars at Papi. The old man retaliates and snatches back his rifle.

'I'm not leaving that boar on the road. I've just shot it. I'm going home to get my van. My friend here will make sure that you don't touch it while I'm gone.'

He stomps off, livid, his dogs trailing behind him. He ignores everything except the dead boar. I catch sight of my neighbours hurrying down the road from Vialanove, towards their vans. The situation is oddly inconclusive. I am not at all sure what has happened. I stare at the bodies, puzzled.

'Why did you shoot the Parisians?'

'Listen to me,' snaps the gendarme, and only then do I realize that it is the same man who stopped me on the motorway, 'if you've got any sense you'll shut up and stop asking questions. We still have to check their real identities. But whoever they were, you're lucky that they didn't shoot you. And they certainly didn't come from Paris.'

He shifts one of the bicycles with his foot. I see the woman's profile, revealed as if for the first time. Her face is unmarked, elegant, her sunburn even and attractive, a gentle spattering of freckles across her nose. The calm, dead face reproaches me with the vanishing charisma of distant cities.

*

'Are you sure they didn't come from Paris? They told us that they did.'

7

MY EMPHASIS: For Mathilde

I am in dispute with my neighbours. This dispute is entirely one-sided. They do not know that I am in dispute with them. The entire affair is all my fault for not checking them out more thoroughly before spending thousands on a picturesque, decrepit cottage. And this particular mixture of guilt, resentment, self-blame and glowing fury is perverse, yet peculiarly English. I have given no outward signs of my displeasure, but I have permitted myself the odd glower and, just once, a slightly brisk slam of the car door. Unrepentant, cheerful, they wave furiously at my goings-out and my comings-in. They have even invited me to drink an aperitif with them. I am considering putting the house back on the market at once. They tell me how wonderful it is to have *'quelqu'un qui médite à côté.'* They never meditate on anything except food. I work all day and feel stricken with various forms of religious guilt if I sit in the sun for half an hour. They spend six hours over a meal without blushing, then invite all their friends round to spend the entire evening doing nothing whatsoever except shouting, giggling or exchanging gossip. And on Friday nights they turn up the music and conduct a jolly fiesta outside my door until two or three in the morning. I am infected with a sort of mad Calvinism. They are not English and I am. They are French.

Is this a conflict of interests, a conflict of lifestyles or a conflict of nations? I cannot decide. Perhaps it's just a conflict of temperaments. Certainly, they appear to be much happier than I am. But they are many, dozens in fact, if you count their visiting satellites, and I am not just few, I am on my own. I talk to the computer, the video, the radio, the TV and the tape. I am writing a play. They talk to each other. If my French was better I could just write them all down. They are all starring in their own family soap: prime-time slots, eight a.m. to around ten – that's breakfast – twelve thirty to three – *le déjeuner* – six thirty onwards for the rest of the night. Fiesta time! On Sundays, they are in continuous performance. Maman, the regular Sunday guest star, drives out to her *lotissement* at Capestang and comes back with her Renault 19 oozing garden produce. Then she settles in before the stove and sink to argue with her daughters-in-law and discuss the family news. The same names always recur. They never appear to work, any of them. I have calculated that they spend fifteen weeks on holiday every year. They never travel or go out of an evening. No, they pass their holidays two feet away from my front windows, laughing and eating. They are all insufferably happy.

I have tried everything. I purchased earplugs and they gave me the hiccups. I closed all the shutters and stifled. I wore earphones and played my own music, but found myself chained to the stereo corner. I slept on the floor of the bathroom and yet I could still hear them. I am con-templating the imminent purchase of a Kalashnikov and have even begun to peruse automatic small-arms cata-logues. This dispute with my neighbours, of which they know nothing, may well turn me into a mass murderer. I will spend the rest of my life in the French equivalent of Spandau. And it will be all their fault.

★

I am the resident playwright for the Morning Glory Theatre Company, of which I am co-founder. Everyone in the company has an equal vote, but the founder's votes carry more weight. In theory, I am very democratic and we are all partners; in practice, I think it only fair that superior experience should be recognized. After all, who fills in the Arts Council grant application forms and oils the wheels on their visits to our premieres? I'm always in the bar, waiting for them, nursing my gin and tonic, while the rest of the company huddles backstage, shit-ting bricks. And it's my work that's on the line too. Don't forget that. It's my dialogue that the cast are busy putting to the slaughter. I think they should damn well listen to me. And by and large they do.

I write one play every year. Sometimes it's a brisk affair – hour and a half – three actors. But sometimes, like this one, I've got all sixteen of them belting it out and then rushing off to get their hats on for the crowd scenes. Put them in hats and overcoats and it always looks like there's more of them. We tour all winter, regular venues, my new play and something by Shakespeare, usually the

A-level set text, and in summer we do the round of the festivals. Or rather they do. That's when I peel off. I am in France, well tanked up on wine and fresh cheese, writing next year's play. I leave the summer tours to George, my co-founder. He hates doing it. But somebody's got to. And there are occasional rewards. They did *The Pirates of Penzance* with an amateur dramatic society, Morning Glory principals of course, and he managed to have sex with a very pretty boy he picked up in the Castle cottage at Aberystwyth.

George isn't what he used to be. He's fifty now, with a natty little paunch. He still has all his hair. I had assumed that the boy had been mistaken about George's age in the dark, but it turned out that the encounter had taken place in full sun and fresh wind on a park bench looking out over the tandoori restaurant that's balanced on the end of the pier. So the boy must have noticed George's stomach dimensions. Dear George, it seems only yesterday that he was playing the young king, Henry V. Now he's masterful as Falstaff.

The boy didn't ask for money either. He settled on a curry dinner and two free tickets for *The Pirates*. George was quite certain that he'd turn up with his boyfriend, and that an evening of sneering and mortification would end with his ulcer acting up and an attack of the vomits. But the boy didn't bring his boyfriend. He came with his mother. George bought them both a drink in the interval, causing a sensation in the bar with his drawn sword and cries of, 'Away there, me hearties.' But he then had to reel back on stage for the second half, with the entire cast of

Morning Glory yelling, 'Who's the girl, George. Who's the girl?' And they didn't mean the mother.

Anyway, let's leave George to it. Summer's here and I'm off to France. I used to rent a Brittany Ferries gîte in years gone by for a whole nine weeks, and paid a special rate. But I got sick of using chipped glasses and uneven sets of cutlery, not knowing how to make the gas work and finding mice in the cupboards. So, after one especially dreadful night with a bolster, which oozed a ghastly trickle of lumpy rags, all mouldered to sawdust, I walked past the Agence Immo in my local town, looked in and then bought a tiny house on the spot for £18,000. It was one of their *invendables* and they were very glad to get it out of the window.

There are many different reasons why houses don't sell quickly, apart from endemic catastrophes like damp rot, termites and the advent of motorways. Either they are too far away from the road or too close, or there's too large a garden or too small a terrace, or the river looks a bit menacing. I used to think that there was a buyer for every house, but I'll never be able to sell this one. The only people who would ever conceivably buy it are the neighbours, and with only one bedroom and a tiny box cupboard upstairs it isn't large enough to become even the minor annexe for them with all their mighty multitudes. Oh, it looked charming enough when I first set eyes upon it. Tucked away in the corner of a romantic medieval square, with a climbing rose draped round the doorway. All original narrow brick façades and no through traffic, two rows of lime trees, crisply shaped, and a marble fountain in the centre which was mentioned in the guidebook. It was Sunday morning and all I could hear were the church bells. I saw it on a February day when the air was chilly and sharp. I told myself that if I liked it in the winter then I would love it in the summer, which is when I would be there for the longest period of time. That's the golden rule with British houses, isn't it? Not so in the South of France. In the summer months you are joined in your rural retreat by most of the inhabitants of Holland, four million Germans, and over half the population of Paris.

My house nestles uneasily into the armpit of the neighbours' edifice. The two properties obviously used to be part of the same building. The umbilical plumbing can't have been very thoroughly separated, because whenever they haul up the button, which they do every twenty seconds or so, a torrent of rushing water descends down just the other side of my sitting-room wall. It's like being perched on the brink of the bowl, waiting to be flushed away. I live with the neighbours all right, and with all their most intimate ablutions. I can hear them washing, farting, yawning, getting into bed and turning out the light. I can hear every word they say.

They don't, however, remain inside the house. This is the Midi and everybody lives outside. The medieval square belongs to the commune and, therefore, theoretically, we all have the right to plonk down our tables and chairs and sit there, guzzling aperitifs until we can no longer tell the difference between black olives and spicy Mexican chips. But in fact, this delightful shady pavement is permanently occupied by an army of squatters: the neighbours.

They have sat there for decades. In fact, their ancestors probably sat there in the Middle Ages. They have acquired that pavement. They're sitting tenants, with every intention of staying put. There was a little flurry of anxiety when I sallied forth early on in the month, armed with a folding deckchair and a book. But I just smiled and nodded amiably. I presented no threat whatsoever. *Que la fête commence!* And so it did, accompanied by music and motorbike arrivals, with flagrant disregard for my artistic concentration. It's not books, it's bums that count. And they have the advantage over me there in terms of sheer numbers of bums. Twelve of them sit down to lunch, day after day. I concede that all is lost and retreat indoors, while bottle after bottle of smoking Ricard goes down their throats. It's not a free country. It's their country. *Vive la France!*

I try to retaliate with a little gentle television. But I watch the Arte programmes, which whisper away in subtitles. They watch American thrillers, in which everybody dies in mass shoot-outs, and an appalling series called *Highlander,* which sports time-travellers in kilts waving supernatural swords, sworn to avenge the McDonalds. My Antonioni season is routed by *Hollywood Night.* I did consider bringing out the heavy guns and spent a fortune on *Götterdämmerung* and a CD player, with thousands of mega watts at my disposal. But, in the end, I am English. I cannot bring myself to disturb their daily celebration, however much they disturb me. So I do what the English always do: I sit behind my net curtains, peering out and hating their guts.

But even the English have their breaking points. One way or another we remember Agincourt and Waterloo. It's in our genes. My patience was vanquished by a babe of four months. And I declared open war. This is how it happened.

Louise and Jean-Yves, the beloved son and tolerated daughter-in-law, arrived from Paris in a Citroën 206, which they installed in my usual parking-place, under a *mûrier,* the only patch of shade left in the square. And there it remained for over a month. I was obliged to leave my car frying beside the fountain. A petty incident, I know, but it rankled. Out of the bowels of their 206 they extracted a purple, yelling infant, which, I gathered, had not travelled well. The rest of the family appeared to experience a sort of religious ecstasy when confronted with its gigantic lung-power and smelly shits. Now I don't know about you, but I loathe children and will not have them in my plays. The parents always mistake early signs of delinquent villainy for genius. Adolescence is a form of torture for its observers rather than its practitioners. When they reach the age of consumption, they get through all your money and everything in the fridge. Their bathroom habits are disgusting. I once briefly acquired a stepdaughter, who dyed the bath aubergine in an attempt to make her mousy locks interesting. But babies – words fail me. I have the good fortune to be born into a culture which hates children even more than I do. Once, when George and I were wearing out our shoes searching for a decent restaurant in Soho that wouldn't push me over my credit-card limit, he lost patience and yelled, 'Whatever's the matter with this one, woman?' And I had to confess that I was looking for that wonderful give-away sign, NO DOGS OR CHILDREN. It's probably banned now, in accordance with EEC rulings. I spend hours at the bar in clip joints, chattering to interesting transvestites of various genders, simply because these places are considered too adult for infants.

Well, anyway, *'le divin enfant'*, the neighbours' last best hope, was much visited by everyone in the locality. I began to recognize the rhythm of astonishment, rapture and *'guhguhguhguh, comme tu es belle, ma petite chérie'*, which rang through my house upon every visit next door. Then, to my horror, the weather, which had been unseasonably showery and cool, suddenly improved. It was 35°C in the shade of the *mûrier*. The babe began teething and was laid outside wearing nothing but a nappy and a tiny little T-shirt, but clearly charged with an obligation to yell itself into hysterics. The creature was now less than two feet away from my white net curtains. I could tell from the key change in the gurgles when she was letting slip the clutch on her lungs and revving herself into the full-volume roar. Out pops Maman to do a bit of expert comforting, all to no avail. The bellowing reaches fever pitch. And as the *petite chérie* was running a temperature, the pitch rose steadily throughout the morning, my quiet working time. By eleven o'clock it was well past all acceptable levels. This went on, day after day. I contemplated sending away to England for that infant wonder drug, Calpol, which one of my exes used to apply to the stepdaughter. Then I became desperate. Cool the thing down, damn you. Then it won't wail without let or hindrance day after day, night after night. Can they really believe that suffering is good for you? I decided to act.

I put all the ice cubes into a large jug, waited until the drops of cold appeared all over the clay surface, then tweaked back the net curtains and poured a little cold water, in reverential baptism, onto the forehead of this wailing mass of pink, fleshy grief. I paint my intentions with the charity of hindsight. At the moment of pouring, I want to drown her. The effect is instantaneous. It must be the shock. The creature's yell is instantly extinguished. She opens her bulging eyes wide and looks up at the hand and the retreating jug. There is a terrible, deathly pause in which heavenly silence engulfs the square, and only the clatter of lunch preparations in the neighbours' kitchen, the odd bump and bang of the pots, disturbs the paradisal quiet. Then the sensation of cold, wet cold, pure as liquid nitrogen, sweeps o'er the tiny beast. Oh, the sublimity of iced water, with its thick, shocking gust of deliciousness. The creature lets fly a shriek that would have brought down Jericho: a single, piercing, dramatic note, the envy of every Italian soprano. Maman, Louise, Jean-Yves, Laurent, Sabine, Bernard and Philippe, who is visiting, arrive on the pavement like The Magnificent Seven.

'Mon Dieu!'

'She's cold and damp all over.'

'Call the doctor!'

'Jean-Yves, how could you have left her alone?'

Very easily. He was attending to his bowels. I could hear every groan.

'*Merde*. She's ill.'

Enclosed by Maman's red scabby grasp, the baby changes tactics. Eyes shut tight, she opens her mouth wide, breathes deep and produces an electrifying howl, which bears the unmistakable aggressive edge of pure rage. I wish I had the gall to howl like that. So unrepentant, resourceful, insistent. What matters? I, me, my, more. Breathe, scream, breathe, scream, breathe, scream, breathe.

This is the theatre of Antonin Artaud, the anti-theatre, the theatre of hate. I cracked.

Quick. Grab your papers. This demoralized mass of dialogue that will never make a play. Quick. Pencils. You always write in pencil. Paper. Loose sheets. Glasses, purse, passport, car keys. You're going back to England, blissful freezing England, where the rain damps down the neighbours, back to your ugly semi-D, where the only sounds you ever hear are the gentle purr of a hovermow or a cat fight in the back garden. Blessed Middle England. Middle-class, middle-aged, middlebrow, where we all hate each other from a decent, respectful distance.

I leap into the car, then out again. The steering wheel has given me a third-degree burn and my bum is on fire. Quick, quick, open up all the windows. Here come the neighbours, intent on lunch and never mind the baby. Shower the driver's seat with water from the fountain. Hypocrite to the last, I smile and wave. Then roar off, shaking with anger and the awful knowledge that I am capable of killing, indeed, I am blissfully capable of mass slaughter. I want to eliminate not just one feeble life, hardly begun, an innocent babe of four months, but an entire tribe. This is the classic pattern of mass murderers. They become semi-reclusive, hardly go out, then suddenly emerge, dressed like the killer on a recent video release, slaughter all their relations and then get going on the neighbours.

I drive like a Formula 1 veteran scaling the Grande Corniche. The little town drops behind me. Here I am amidst the red earth and white rock of a country that I love. Here are the vines, green, green, huge clustered bunches of green, fat with possibility. There is the river, shrinking in the heat, the weed steadily drying as the rocks raise their backs from the cold, swirling rush. And here is the next little town, looming up behind a shivering row of poplars.

CESSENON-SUR-ORB, son église du XIIIe siècle, ses remparts. Camping municipal troisième rue à gauche. Fête locale 5/6 et 7 juillet. Marchés: mardi, vendredi et dimanche matin devant l'église. HÔTEL DU MIDI**, ses plats gastronomiques régionaux, Place de la Révolution ...

Everything shimmers in the heat. I hear the squish of my tyres on melting asphalt. Then here we are in a giant cave of green, the *Place de la Révolution* with everyone quietly eating at little tables under the trees.

I have left everything behind. Cheque book, credit cards, Channel tunnel tickets, toothbrush, all my clothes. I haven't even locked the front door. I am hungry enough to eat the offending baby. I screech to a halt.

My entrance into the small, shadowy dining room of the Hôtel du Midi causes a minor sensation. My grey hair is standing on end and I am cowering inside a purple T-shirt, with a huge sunflower traversing my enormous bosoms, encircled with the slogan MORNING GLORY. I look like Percy Thrower's Dream. My arms are filled with pencils, a scrabbled mass of papers, half a dozen floppy discs, a massive dog-eared volume of *The Complete Works of Shakespeare,* which now looks like a rucksack book. I have no handbag and am wearing two different espadrilles, one black, one red. I am also half an hour late for lunch. Everyone else in the dining room eats there every day. They even have their own tables and napkins. They have almost finished their *escalope de veau à la crème,* with either chips or *pommes de terre dauphine* and a *salade verte.* They are eating with their husbands, his sister, maman, all their mates from work, or the colleague from Nantes, who is here for *'quatre jours'.* They have all stopped talking and are looking at me. Freeze-frame. Ready? Yes. Action.

Madame oozes smoothly across the tiles, both eyebrows raised.

'I hope I'm not too late for lunch,' I declaim in my breathtaking French.

'Ah, no.'

Madame is a magnificent bottle blonde, once ravishing. She has the most extraordinary grey eyes. She is now well past her best as the belle of the village, but is on her way to the next stage. She is becoming gorgeous, powerful, sensuous, married but passionately sought after. Everybody wants to be her lover. She is the resident *étoile* of the Hôtel du Midi. Peering round a column is a ten-year-old child who must be her daughter. They have the same eyes.

I am ushered to my table halfway down the room. As I walk the length of this lunchtime stage, all eyes are upon me, and I remember, vividly, why I gave up acting. But, if I can no longer write plays, and so far this summer I have written nothing whatsoever that we can use, because of the neighbouring fiesta, I may well find myself back on the boards and Morning Glory will be performing something unspeakable by Tom Stoppard. By the time Madame sits me down, I am near to tears. Every single person in the restaurant notices that the mad Englishwoman with the electric hair and the lurid T-shirt is about to collapse, weeping. Madame smoothes the marbled linen and her voice drops an octave.

'*Voilà*. You will have lots of space for your papers.' Her murmur suggests the ultimate caress. I fight back the flood of wretchedness, frustration and relief.

'Thank you,' I sniffle carefully. Madame glitters with reassurance and sympathy. 'Thank you. You see, I couldn't write at home. And I must write. I have to write. I was prevented from writing. I'm a writer. I didn't mean any harm. But I couldn't help myself . . .'

And then I let slip the fatal phrase, that innocent mistake, which I now hold responsible for everything else that happened that summer, *'Enfin, j'ai dû partir de chez moi.'* I am on the run from home.

The entire restaurant shudders with a wave of indignant sympathy. *'La pauvre dame . . . c'est intolérable. Heureusement elle est partie . . . Tiens, la même chose est arrivée chez ma cousine. . .'* I bask in the pink glow of solidarity. At last, I have come home. I nod to my companions. My *oeuf mayonnaise* arrives, yellow, creamy, desperately fattening and home made. I am looking into a young sunburned face, with long, dark-gold hair and grey eyes. She smiles but says nothing. At last, an utterly silent child. I beam back.

'Comment tu t'appelles, toi?'

'Mathilde.'

'Bonjour, Mathilde.'

'Et vous?'

'Henri.'

'C'est un nom de garçon.'

'It's short for Henrietta.'

'I will call you Stylo. Because you're a writer.'

Stylo means biro. I'm not too keen on being called a biro.

'But I write with pencils. Maybe you ought to call me *"crayon"*.'

'You don't look like a pencil. *Tant pis.* Give me your pencils. I'll sharpen them upstairs. And then you can write.'

We have made friends.

The entire restaurant supports my choice of fish, my bottle of rosé, my iced water. They approve my request for a local cheese as it descends with a whiff of goat. They enjoy my delight in the *tarte aux prunes,* made by Mathilde's grandmother, who appears in the doorway to view the new arrival. I am on my second *café* and well into the first scene of the second act when Madame appears to ask me if all is well.

'Ah, I feel very much better.'

'These things happen.'

'Alas, they do.'

'I hope that you can mend the fences.'

'Well, I don't think I can. But at least I didn't start shouting.'

It is very French and perfectly permissible to shout. But it doesn't come to me that easily. We stand shaking our heads in perfect agreement.

'So nothing irreversible has actually been said.'

'Oh no. I wouldn't have done that.'

'But it was bad enough that you had to leave home.'

'I don't know why I haven't cracked before. It's been like this for weeks.'

'Weeks!'

Madame is incredulous.

'Ever since I've been there really. I had no idea. You make a commitment in good faith and then . . .'

Madame lowers her voice. We are women together, talking about intimate women's things.

'Do you need a room at the Hôtel?'

'Oh no.' I smile grimly. 'It hasn't come to that yet. But it may do.'

'Does he know where you are?'

And suddenly, with a flash of horror, I realize why the restaurant has been so magnificently sympathetic. *I am a battered wife.* The whole scenario unmasked, revealed, is played out before me, like a pop-up comic book. I am a woman of a certain age. My sentimental life might have been considered decently buried. But no! Romance unfurled its silver wings. I was swept off my feet and into a Mediterranean love nest, when suddenly the real face of Midi Machismo illuminated the brute's moustache as he reached for the bottle and the whip. Wait till I get George on the blower. He'll laugh himself into producing a litter of kittens. But what on earth can I say to this generous, wonderful, opulent bottle blonde? Who is looking into my eyes with such loving concern that I am in danger of forgetting my role. Panic. Quick. Speak the lines.

'You are very kind. But no, I don't think so. I'll go home tonight. I have to try to make it work. After all, it's my house.'

'*Votre maison. Ah, bien.* I understand. *Mais écoutez* . . . if he won't let you write and you must write . . . Come here. I can give you a table and you can stay the whole afternoon. Once we've cleared lunch we don't use the dining room. It's very cool.'

I have a study. A silent, pleasant study with a vaulted ceiling and stone niches burrowed deep into the walls, a study that figures in the guidebooks and has two stars in the Michelin, a study in the little village of Cessenon-sur-Orb. Madame and I shake hands and gaze fervently into one another's eyes. There is justice on this earth. There is a God. Rejoice.

Mathilde appears at my elbow. She stands there, just looking. I think that one of my reasons for disliking children so intensely is that they are all a little uncanny. Their faces are often impassive, their thoughts cannot be interpreted or even imagined by the external world. They have neither ethics nor morals. These things are never innate. They are always acquired. But this child does not make me feel uncomfortable. She is on my side. And here she stands, companionable, friendly, holding out a sheaf of sharpened pencils.

'Would you like a *thé citron*? It might be more refreshing than another *petit café*.'

Good God, she talks like an adult.

'Thank you, Mathilde. I would.'

She delivers the tall glass of tea in a Russian-style silver holder, placing it on the table before me with immense concentration. Once it is safe she stands still again, looking at me, not at my writing.

'Would you like to see what I've written?'

'I haven't started English yet.'

We pause. I look at her. She looks at me. We are both overcome by a more confiding mood.

'Will your husband kill you?' Mathilde enquires pleasantly. 'Maman says that often happens.'

'He may do. But he isn't my husband. He's only a visiting lover.'

'Maman has one of those. Papa doesn't mind. He's her cousin.'

I am slightly stunned by this piece of information, but very encouraged.

'I hope he never hits Maman.'

'Oh, never. Neither does Papa. They both like her. Why doesn't your lover like you?'

Good question. I haven't yet invented this part of the plot and I'm in deep water now. My desperate expression is misinterpreted by Mathilde's generosity.

'Don't be sad. It will all get better soon. Why don't you have your tea?'

She pats my arm like a professional hostess and vanishes. Later, she returns with a large exercise book, scored across with faint blue squares. She settles down opposite with her own stash of coloured pencils and begins to draw. We work away in companionable silent concentration. By the end of the afternoon Mathilde presents me with a coloured portrait of myself, writing. My Morning Glory sunflower is coloured in luminous yellow, my hair in wild, rigid punk spikes. I'll have it framed.

The *thé citron* does not appear on the bill, but when I mention this, Madame is emphatic.

'Ah no. That was a present from Mathilde to her new friend. She made it herself. She explained that it was for you.'

I bow very graciously and look round for Mathilde, but she has mysteriously disappeared. In fact, she is waiting by my car to say goodbye.

'*A demain?*' she asks hopefully, peering in at the mess of tapes and books on the floor.

'*Mais oui. C'est promis. Midi et demi.* Have my table ready.'

I ring George that night, full of my adventures and the fact that I am now a victim of male oppression. George doesn't believe that this is possible. He thinks that women are all like Goneril and Regan, plotting atrocities, and i' the heat. He also thinks that beneath that nice-as-pie-goody-two-shoes-act, Cordelia is as bloody-minded as the sadistic sisters. But he's happy to concede that all men are bastards, for this reflects his own amorous experiences. I wouldn't know. Men aren't my thing. But he's right about the girls.

Down from the waist they're centaurs,
Though women all above.
But to the girdle do the gods inherit;
Beneath is all the fiends.
There's hell, there's darkness, there is the sulphurous pit . . .

And so on. True, my dears, all true. George interrupts me to say he hopes that the new play is a comedy, as the *King Lear* rehearsals are taking it out of him something terrible. I promise to sweeten my imagination by every means available.

And so it all begins. I get quite a bit of work done in the afternoons. Mathilde hammers away at her *devoirs de vacances* perched opposite. The play takes shape.

But back in the burning square, eight kilometres away, the daily fiesta takes on new dimensions. This is partly because of the heat. Our houses are invaded by flies and a Babel's tower of mini-bugs circles under the main lampshade. By eleven o' clock in the morning the walls breathe out the damp. The washing is dry within minutes and there is no consoling wind. The old ladies in black on the other side of the square sit clamped to their chairs in the ancestral shade, but ease their feet gently out of their tartan wool slippers. The whole earth around us gasps for air. The river runs dry. Only a few dank puddles are left in the deeper fissures of the gorge. The neighbours move all their household goods out onto the pavement directly in front of my windows. They set light to their barbecue. A dark cloud of delicious smoking smells rushes into my sitting room. More, yes more of them arrive from Marseilles, explaining that the apartment is no longer *vivable*. The streets of the city are melting. How fortunate that they can all escape to the peaceful medieval square and the everlasting arms of the family. They balance the television on the window sill, so that they can continue to enjoy *Highlander* and *Hollywood Night* while breathing the thin wisps of air that pass through the spray of the fountains. The content of their domestic conversation is reduced to the heat, how each one of them is bearing up and what on earth they should eat given the rising temperature. Even the cheese is confined to the fridge. Speculations about a coming thunderstorm provide the only variation in their daily round of clichés.

The children become cross, exhausted, lethargic. The baby becomes unbearable. I am privileged to hear every long, devastating whinge and their irritating refusals to take up any of Maman's intelligent suggestions. Their favourite bathing pool is now dry. There are too many other people at the *piscine*. It's too hot to even contemplate the car. *'Alors, la plage. C'est hors de question . . . Maman, Maman, Maman, j'en ai marre . . .'*

The new arrivals from Marseilles are very curious to see what the mad Englishwoman has done to the house, which once belonged to Uncle Jules and should, of course, never have left the family. A long wail over the evils of the French inheritance system follows. I have heard all this before. Families are sundered for ever as a result. Would that they were. This tribe is held together by superglue and general hatred of the late Uncle Jules, who is the convenient scapegoat. Has *la voisine* put in central heating? The Maison Jules was always very damp. They peer in through my thick net curtains. Hmm? I am discussed in general terms, all perfectly audible, as *la voisine anglaise*. But when Maman says complacently, 'Oh, we don't see a lot of her, she's very quiet,' I am ready to kick in the television.

But of course I don't do it. Instead, I cower in the bathroom, the only room that does not have a window onto the square, and smoke two cigarettes, before slinking out through the back door into a narrow smelly passage which stinks of rampant toms. How can I recover my car and drive off without being obliged to smile and wave at these monsters of egotism?

I know this may sound unreasonable and dotty, but I have begun to resent the neighbours even more now that I am getting some work done in the afternoons. I resent the fact that, even when I get up early and manage a page or two before breakfast, I am forced back into teeth gnashing frustration for the entire morning until I can leave for lunch. I resent the very modest seventy francs a day, which I pay at the Hôtel du Midi. Why can't I eat at home? But most of all, I resent the nightmare evenings of trivial chatter and bad music. Families have no idea how boring their conversation is to outsiders. Especially to those who don't wish to hear it. I wish that I could not understand a single word of French. Then at least I would be spared the endless discussion of the late Uncle Jules, his appalling death, *le baptême* of the *divin enfant,* the forthcoming marriage of Sophie to Jean-Pierre, whoever they are, and what on earth would they all do if Laurent went to Canada? If I couldn't understand it the whole thing would be one long irritating burble, not a personal affront to my privacy. By the end of the first week into the heatwave I am ready to buy Laurent's ticket myself. At least that would be one of them packed off and gone for good.

I cannot read. I cannot sleep. I cannot bear it any more.

George sends me a videotape of Morning Glory's *King Lear.* He is playing Kent. They have made a daring production decision and are apparently doing it straight, in traditional Elizabethan costume, a grandiose dramatic style, lots of props and painted sets, real sword fights, doublet and hose with matching codpiece. Men in tights. I gasp. They must have used up all next year's costume budget. George is clearly basing his barnstorming performance on Peter O'Toole's memorable *Macbeth*. I knew that it was going to be controversial when Gloucester tickled Kent's penis in the opening scene to make his meaning perfectly clear. Almost everyone loses their temper, accompanied by a violent fit of shouting in the first act. Lear breaks Cordelia's teeth, smashes all the props and threatens to slit Kent's throat. I sit, mesmerized and appalled, as Cordelia goes for her sisters' faces with bright red polished talons, before spitting, literally, at her hapless suitors and then making off for France. This is *King Lear* as family quarrel, gloves off.

For a moment I am home again with my own theatre company, utterly engrossed.

Then the neighbours begin singing.

It is somebody's birthday, a family fête. And somebody else, somebody visiting, has either been married, baptized or swallowed their first communion.

'Jean-Yves, une chanson! Jean-Yves, une chanson! Jean-Yves, une chanson!'

And their fists hit the table in rhythmic demand. Jean-Yves has an unspeakable guitar. Twaaaang. Here come the first chords, announcing his electric approach.

That's it. I lose it completely.

I cannot kick the television in because there, upon the screen, close up and yelling, is George, ready to carve Oswald into rare beef slices. So I turn up the volume to Mark 10 and George is left bellowing:

'Thou whoreson zed! thou unnecessary letter! My lord, if you will give me leave, I will tread this unbolted villain into mortar and daub the walls of a jakes with him. Help, ho! Murder! Murder! Help!'

I go for the washing machine, then all the pans and crockery, in a sequence of horrifying crashes. Who cares? It's all junk from Champion. George keeps me company, roaring his head off.

'A plague upon your epileptic visage!
Smile you upon my speeches, as I were a fool?
Goose, if I had you upon Sarum Plain
I'd drive ye cackling home to Camelot.'

I sweep everything off the worktop and screech at the top of my voice, drowning Oswald completely,

'What, art thou mad, old fellow?'

The garlic crusher hurtles into the sink, smashing two glasses. Wielding an empty wine bottle, I attack the cupboards, bop the telephone and the Minitel in passing, and then pause in my domestic rampage to fling the entire neatly stacked collection of little logs, one by one, into the fireplace. Crash! Heave! Thump! Crash!

'Call not your stocks for me,' George thunders from the telly, now in full fustian blast, *'I serve the King.'* My living room lies destroyed in heaps around me. I fling myself upon the telly zapper. George vanishes and dead silence reigns within and beyond the shutters.

My hurricane of rage has blown itself out in four minutes precisely. I lie doggo. I hear a faint rustle and whispering from the neighbours. They are moving indoors, or away to their cars? I cannot believe it. It cannot be. This is too beautiful. They are going inside. Alleluia! I sit triumphant amidst the chaos of smashed plates and gently vibrating pots. Jubilant, I pour myself a drink.

But, twenty minutes later, when I am well into my second Scotch, peacefully listening to a Bach cello suite on the CD, which I have had the sense not to demolish, there is a stout rap upon the front door. Oh God, I can guess who it is. And yes, indeed, there she is, face set, arms folded. Maman!

I have no idea what I look like, but my room has clearly been taken apart by a gang of mad burglars. And here I stand, red and shaky, clutching the whisky bottle in one hand and a hefty slug of alcohol in the other. Maman surveys the wreckage with a darkening countenance. There is no one else there, but she is nobody's fool. They had all heard a man's voice, raging in English.

'Did he get out by the back door?' she cries, putting her arm around me. 'Are you all right? Should I ring the SAMU?'

I then notice that she is carrying a heavy pewter ladle in one hand and that Jean-Yves, now wielding a hammer rather than his guitar, has appeared in the doorway just behind her.

'Call the children,' snaps Maman, 'we must help our *voisine* clear this up.'

I never did find out what happened to Papa, the patriarchal gender partner of this formidable woman, but he must have died of her decisiveness. Now they are no longer outside but in my living room, *la grande armée,* wielding mops and dustpans. I lie quivering on the sofa, mouthing, *'Mercy, mercy,'* like an expiring fish. Maman pours herself a Scotch and pats my arm with her magnificent, well-chapped paw. *'C'est fini, c'est fini,'* she promises consolingly, as if I were an injured child. Nobody, thank God, suggests that we should call the police.

★

Next day, Mathilde is waiting for me on the restaurant terrace. Her face lights up with relief as she sees my car pulling into the square. And she bounds across the road, tail in the air like a golden retriever.

'Stylo! Stylo! Are you OK?' She pulls me down to her level and gives me a kiss. 'He was back again, wasn't he? Don't worry. You are quite safe here. I'll protect you.'

Mathilde is now standing before me, a knight of the Jedi, waving her sword of retractable light. I am so struck by the charm of this child, protecting an old woman three times her size, that I do not think to ask how she knows that the lover from hell has put in another appearance. But the whole restaurant knows. As we march in together there is a little burst of applause from the regulars and a fascinated stare from four baffled Dutch tourists.

'*Ah, madame, bravo.*'

'*Il est parti? Espérons . . .*'

'*C'est incroyable.*'

'*Il ne vous a pas fait mal . . . ?*'

'*Prenez votre apéritif avec nous . . .*'

The restaurant settles down to pick over the eternal problem of domestic violence. They are working with a broad set of definitions. Do you remember old Pinson? Yes, him. He used to beat the living daylights out of his *pauvre fils,* until the boy ran off, and high time too. And Jean-Jacques from Rieussac, just like his brother, who

204

never laid a finger on his wife, but carried an axe in his belt at all times and waved it at her whenever she didn't agree with him. The stories of women's methods of domestic repression are rarer, but more devious. Madame Tullot got her sister to sign over the land by threatening to poison her drinks. And old Camille Deroux, what a witch! Thank God she's dead. She whipped her son's testicles if he didn't stack the wood properly and that's what made him a homosexual. One woman has an extraordinary story of a boyfriend who lifted her clear off the ground at la Gare du Nord in Paris and banged her against the wall until an old gentleman tottered up and told him to put her down, it's not polite to bang women against walls. And the boyfriend, who was a soldier out of uniform, had snapped out of it, dropped her in a heap and saluted. His *service militaire* took over at the key moment. And Nicole – that's Mathilde's mum, we're now tu-toi-ing each other like mad – told us all about her *voisine,* who was much younger than her man – he was fifty and she was twenty-five – but they both drank as much as the other and, well, things got hot, and she took his gun down from the wall and men- aced him with both barrels. It was loaded, so he didn't argue. He got out of the house somehow and came round to use Nicole's phone. Then the girl started firing rounds out of the window, but she hadn't run out of ammunition when the police got there and there was a siege situation with a negotiator using a loud-hailer, but the girl was off her head and didn't talk sense, so they had to wait until she passed out with a crash. Then they stormed the building in bullet-proof vests, and it was all over the front page of the *Midi Libre* the next morning, DOMESTIC SIEGE ENDS WITHOUT BLOODSHED, and she still has the cutting.

But as for giving the wife the odd clout round the ears, well, almost every Frenchman does it at some time or another. And that doesn't count really, does it? Not so long as you give as good as you get.

Everyone agrees that my irate lover is jealous of my writing and that's his motive. The clientele at the restaurant never ask questions. They make statements. So all I have to do is smile and nod. I decide that the itinerant source of their information must be *la boulangère,* who trundles round all the villages which don't have a bakery. She's a real *bavarde,* the *boulangère,* and she tells a good story.

Mathilde and I are a little blocked that afternoon, given all the excitement. But she eventually illustrates the tale of Madame Tullot and her sister, with the old hag dressed in black lace, carrying a sinister green drink. I spend a lot of time dreaming up another plot twist which involves rewriting a previous scene. I never plot my plays completely from start to finish. I have a general idea, but I leave lots of room for manoeuvre. And I like my characters to surprise me. That makes it all the more interesting.

'Do you think her sister lay in bed the whole time?' asks Mathilde after an hour of tranquil scratching.

'Whose sister?'

'Madame Tullot's sister, of course.'

'Oh yes, she was ground to a shadow of her former self,' I assert peacefully as we reflect on all the stories, their shapes and nuances.

King Lear is, after all, just a family drama with cosmic implications. There's something there which echoes all the domestic catastrophes of Cessenon-sur-Orb: axe-waving, father against son, poisonings and shoot-outs. The people you hate most are the ones you see every day. But your family can't be sacked like your colleagues. They may walk out, break it off, refuse to speak to you, cut you out of their wills, ignore you in the street, but always, when you see them face to face, pale with rage, the cut of her jaw, the line of his paunch, the way she looks just like Aunt Susie used to do at her age, all those tiny things, written in blood and bone, reproach your denial. Somewhere or other, Mathilde knows this. As she passes the definitive illustration of *Madame Tullot's Murder* across the table I notice that she has given the sisters the same face.

But what is family after all? Who are family? Look at me. I don't have a family. There's Jerry in America, I suppose, but he never writes. I hear what's happened once a year when his wife includes a note on the Christmas card. She always asks when Morning Glory is going to sail across the pond and tour the States. Tour the States? We're lucky if we get invited to tour Leeds, Bradford and Sheffield. The nearest we ever get to the West End is the Hampstead Everyman. But if I have a family anywhere it's Morning Glory. We all talk about founding a family, don't we? Well, I'm the founder of that one.

Not that we don't all fall out from time to time. There was that night in Exeter when James pushed Valeria over the steps at Ye Olde Shippe Inne and she broke her ankle. She did the whole show on crutches. And the audience stood up to cheer her curtain calls. But she didn't speak to James for the entire three weeks, except on stage. And given that he was her leading man, it was all a bit tricky. Then there was the row George and I had about doing musicals. If anything's a crowd-puller, it's a musical. Especially one that the audience already knows. I just couldn't understand his resistance. He never made that kind of fuss about the pantomime. I was dead set on *South Pacific* as a summer show. After all, as I pointed out, he was used to coconut breasts every Christmas as one of the Ugly Sisters, and as for the songs! *'There is nothing like a dame . . .'* George! It's you! I wouldn't let up. We had one blazing row in front of the entire company. Two of them burst into tears. It was as if they'd caught their parents fighting. We had to kiss and make up then and there to calm them down. *South Pacific* was a roaring success and not even George could keep up a sulk in front of a packed house.

Yes, if I have a family at all it's Morning Glory. And if I have a partner it's George. We've been together thirty years and it's as loving a friendship as I've ever had or could ever want. There's never been anything sexual. George is queer and that's that. Me, I'm neither one thing nor the other, and I can't say I've ever been in love apart from the odd crush on women twice my age. I've loved the Company and the life we've led, the company of my Company, if you see what I mean.

But I'm getting very fond of this big-bosomed bottle-blonde hotel manager and her grey-eyed daughter. Mathilde now always brings her lunch in and eats with me. Eating is a social thing. Morning Glory always eat together. You should always eat with your family.

Well, for a few weeks or so after the Big Smash Up, things went quiet next door. They clearly thought I needed time to recover. It was so hot that Laurent took all the young ones off to the beach every day and they sat inside when they came home, nursing their sunburn and moaning. I made up a tape of George shouting. Just the highlights from Act I and Act II, with a little bit of James as the King himself, calling up the cataracts and hurricanoes. He did that speech awfully well, with a lot of clenched fists and stamping. Splice *King Lear* carefully together and you get one long domestic row at full volume. I thought I'd use the tape again if the noise from next door became insupportable. I'd left a few gaps for me to pitch in, shrieking: 'RHUBARB! RHUBARB!' if necessary. It's very hard to be intolerably loud on your own, but with a little technological support from Morning Glory and the Bard I had a family dust-up of biblical proportions, all prepared.

Then the one thing happened which I hadn't foreseen. The neighbours had a row. It began just before lunch-time. I wasn't following, but I heard the tone change between Maman and Louise. The older woman said something sharp and Louise flounced off into the house. There was a horrible pause. I sauntered past, on my way to Cessenon, trying not too obviously to gloat. My cheerful and malicious *'Bon appétit'* was greeted with a row of curt nods.

Well, it must have simmered away all afternoon, while Mathilde and I were covering sheets of paper in the dark cave of our deserted restaurant, because by the time I got home at nine thirty they were all at each other's throats. Laurent was sitting outside on his own, twiddling two forks, his face black with rage. And in the kitchen, with all the doors open, Maman was in full swing. She was the heavy artillery. Louise and Sabine, the daughters-in-law, were keeping up a steady blast of small-arms fire. Every so often the men sent in an old-fashioned cannon ball with flames attached, but these were more or less discounted in the context of modern family warfare. The row was between the women. I couldn't get a handle on the issues. But this is always true of other people's quarrels.

No one listening to me and George squabbling about *South Pacific* would have understood the deeper implications. George wants Morning Glory to have a serious profile and a reputation for innovative versions of classic drama. I want bums on seats. He wants us to be controversial and intellectual. I want us to be entertainers. He wants *King Lear* and I want *Some Enchanted Evening*. We both got our own way in the end I suppose. We just do different things for different publics. And the critics, when they bother to take any notice of us at all, praise us for our 'diversity'. What they're praising is an uneasy family compromise.

No compromise next door. Maman isn't going to give way on her own turf. Not bloody likely. The entire square sits mesmerized by the yelling. Ah, Louise has stormed off upstairs. The baby has woken up and is roaring. I can hear everything. Yes, down come the suitcases from the top of the wardrobe. She is going back to Paris. Jean-Yves has rushed up the stairs. He is trying to dissuade her. Sabine is howling the French equivalent of look what you've gone and done at Maman. Laurent rises up. He is bellowing through the kitchen window. I close my own front windows carefully and open the back door. But there is no excluding the neighbours. This will go on all night.

Time to throw in my tuppence worth. I raise my voice in a dramatic yell, 'Stop! I said stop! That's enough!' And fling the switch on the tape.

'Be Kent unmannerly when Lear is mad? What wouldst thou do, old man?

Thinkst thou that duty shall have dread to speak
When power to flattery bows?'

The text is even quite appropriate. Louise is the youngest daughter-in-law. She is getting a faceful of abuse from Maman, which she doesn't deserve. Maman thinks that no woman is good enough for her precious sons. And that bloody baby has made it all worse. Maman tells both girls how to behave as if they were clueless bimbos. I've heard her do it. Louise has never been so close to a baby before and now she's got one of her own. Of course she's going to get things wrong from time to time. Mothering isn't a natural process. You have to learn it, bottle by nappy. But Maman is always right. Or at least she always thinks she is. And that doesn't help.

I join George in yelling:

'Thy youngest daughter does not love thee least,
Nor are those empty-hearted whose low sounds
Reverb no hollowness.'

Not that Louise is going in for low sounds. She has flung open the upstairs window and is yelling abuse about Maman into the square. I turn up the tape and hit my Act II selection of invective at a competitive pitch. Then, seized with theatrical gusto, I make my next fatal mistake. I am standing in the middle of my sitting room, waving my arms and shouting at a whirling cassette. My elbow catches a vase of carnations and sends them spinning off the breakfast bar. That's it. At the first smash of crockery, Jean-Yves, Laurent and Maman are hammering at the door. I lunge for the tape, slip in the water on the floor and go flying. I just have time to silence the tape, so that as the neighbours burst into the room I am discovered lying flat on my stomach in front of my machines, nursing a bleeding forearm which has been gouged by a random piece of splintered vase. Someone has their arms around me and is giving me a huge hug. Good God, it is Mathilde.

'Stylo! Are you OK?' She is very sweet and serious. Maman is directing operations.

'Quick! He went out the back door.' Mercifully, incriminatingly, this stands open.

Laurent and Jean-Yves are heard thundering away down the smelly back passage. I expect to hear yells of 'Stop Thief' at any moment.

'Stylo's bleeding,' says Mathilde to Maman, utterly matter-of-fact.

But of course Maman has bandages and tincture of iodine. In the blessed calm, which always follows catastrophe, I hear the baby's howl reduced to a faint grizzle. The carnations splattered all over the floor make the disaster look much worse than it actually is. Mathilde collects up all the flowers, her pink plastic sandals skidding perilously in the pools on the tiles. I sit down on my sofa and concentrate on getting my breath back.

'Mathilde! What on earth are you doing here?'

'Visiting my cousins. But it turned out to be a bad idea. They're all angry with each other today.'

I knew it. Maman and Nicole are sisters. I should have expected this. The buggers are all related. Well, thank God I never slagged off the neighbours in the resto. It would all have got back. I feel surrounded by the enemy and put my head in my hands. But Mathilde, who has proved again and again that she is on my side, sits down peacefully and says,

'Don't be sad. He's gone.'

We look at one another. For quite different reasons we are both very relieved. Mathilde looks around my sitting room, staring at each object in turn.

'I like your house,' she says, 'it's much nicer than it was when Uncle Jules lived here.' I am pleased by this, but as I find out to my cost, Mathilde is one of those children who never misses anything. And who remembers.

Maman and Louise are both here, temporarily reconciled and in disaster-management mode. They both examine my cut. I discover that Louise is a nurse at Villejuif.

'I do cancers, not cuts,' she explains, 'but I can see that this doesn't need stitches. It's quite clean. Here, Maman, I'll put two of these plasters on the wound. They'll hold the cut closed. It'll heal by itself. *Voilà*!'

At last! Louise has an expertise that is recognized and praised. Maman catches herself saying, 'My daughter-in-law is a fully qualified nurse. You can be quite reassured.'

I am, I am. Oh God.

Maman is sitting down opposite. She is going to *faire la morale*. I can see it coming.

'*Ecoutez,*' she begins. 'I know that it's none of my business, but it seems to me that this man is not good to you. He isn't making you happy and he only comes to cause trouble. If you say the word, I'll tell my boys to keep him away. He usually comes in the evenings, right?'

Laurent and Jean-Yves have found Bernard, who was skulking in a café. All three of them come heaving through the back door. They think they saw him get away. I am flabbergasted by this announcement.

'He drives a Citroën, doesn't he?'

'Um? Yes, I think he does.'

'A green one?'

'Er, yes, sort of.'

'Damn. We didn't get the number.'

'But we're on the watch now.'

'What does he look like?'

'Er?'

'That's him,' cries Mathilde with uncanny accuracy and plucks a cherished photograph off the television. It is indeed a photo of George and I, hugging one another on the set of *South Pacific*. 'Happy talking, happy talking, happy talk, / Talk about things you like to do / You've got to have a dream / If you don't have a dream / How you gonna have a dream come true?' Oh God, there we are, surrounded by coconut palms and Morning Glory, all camping it up as American sailors. The neighbours study the photograph carefully. George is fully made up, sporting a wig, naked to the waist, with a long grass skirt and a floral garland draped over coconut falsies and his hairy chest. I look pretty much as I always do: bright purple T-shirt and spiky hair. And there is James in the front row of sailors, pretending to do the horn-pipe. *Merde*.

'I'm the artistic director of a theatre company,' I mumble helplessly.

'*Ah, c'est pour ça . . .*'

'*Bien.*'

'*C'est sur scène . . .*'

'*Il est acteur.*'

Yes, God help us all, he's an actor.

'We'll find him. We'll stop him,' declares Jean-Yves decisively.

★

August arrives with a barrage of thunderstorms. We are all forced to hover inside our tinkling bamboo door screens and watch the torrents flooding the square. I am well into the finale of Act III and the play is going great guns. The boys are consumed with purpose despite the bad weather. They have formed a posse of vigilantes and taken to patrolling the back passage with their baseball caps pulled low and their anorak collars turned up. They tap the door regularly with a reassuring:

'On est là, Madame!'

I call back, *'Merci, Laurent; merci, Jean-Yves; merci, Bernard.'*

They have purchased coshes and balaclavas for the night patrols and are clearly enjoying themselves enormously. The universal approbation of our tiny village falls upon them and copious sympathy upon me. There is even a line or two about the affair under 'Local Comment' in the *Midi Libre*. I feel no guilt whatsoever. I am at last part of the community.

Now that the heat has broken Mathilde and I begin to go out on trips in the late watery afternoons. So far she has shown me the Mediterranean gardens and the Cathar Martyrs Memorial Museum. I have got to know both Nicole's husband and her lover. They too are pledged to carve my violent actor into little pieces should he ever dare to show his face again. There is a vague muttering in the kitchen about how the Anglais don't know how to treat women. Given the tales of domestic horror that are recounted here I don't think that the Channel counts for much.

The show must go on. But the one person to whom I say nothing, despite the fact that I speak to him every night, is, of course, George.

'Sounds like you're getting on better with your neighbours,' he comments amiably during one of our nightly calls. '*King Lear* is doing very well. James will fax you our bundle of excellent reviews. We're very thrilled, my dear. You should be proud of us all.'

I coo agreeable noises down the line.

The fax arrives bearing kilometres of good reviews. I read them as they emerge from the machine, very pleased. But at the end of the pleasure marathon comes an alarming punchline. A jubilant note from George.

Hello old thing!

Wonderful news. The Narbonne Festival du Théâtre en Plein Air have invited us to replace Harry's Actor's Theatre Company at short notice. They're all on strike apparently. The focus is on Shakespeare. Beat this: ***L'Homme, ses pièces, sa signification universelle***! And they want Morning Glory's *King Lear.* The Festival runs from 17–28 August and we're on in the second week; union rates and all expenses paid. We're being put up in the Hôtel du Lion d'Or, details to follow. I'll come down early to set things up. Can you meet me at Montpellier?

All love and hugs, George

Union Rates! The Festival Committee must have subsidy money coming out of its ears. At all costs, I must keep George out of the village. Narbonne is barely thirty kilometres away. No problem. He'll be too busy getting the show up and running in the amphitheatre, or wherever they're performing, and putting everybody through their voice tests. I have three stiff drinks then fax back.

> My Dearest George
> Bravo to you and the Company for the King Lear Reviews. Fax me your ETOA at Montpellier. I am assuming that Morning Glory will come down in the truck and the camper.
> All my Love Henry

Don't panic. No one need ever know. Have another stiff drink. Turn on the television. Relax.

★

In the end family is what counts, isn't it? I am reunited with my family in the foyer of the Lion d'Or amidst the mirrors, fake gilt and potted palms. We fall into one another's arms, shrieking.

'Henry! Let's take a look at you, darling!'
'How's the play?'
'I say, you *have* put on weight!'
'Is there a good part for me?'
'Did you see the *King Lear* reviews?'
'You're not at all brown.'

'Is it always this hot?'

'How's the new house?'

'Valeria's got a headache. Do they sell Nurofen?'

'Jimmy's performance was described as "definitive" in the *Sunday Telegraph*.'

'I ate some of that cheese and now I feel sick.'

'Oh God, how I've missed you all.'

'Well, it's you that swans off and leaves us all summer, you jammy bugger.'

★

The open-air amphitheatre is constructed inside the empty core of the old cathedral. Normally it's a car park. The cathedral was never finished because in order to construct the nave the builders would have had to demolish the town walls. Apparently, the Black Prince and his army were standing just outside, itching to get in. So all that remains are the giant soaring Gothic chapels and pillars with the perfect floating shafts of the windows, all pulling up, up, up to the roofless vault. And above, nothing but scorching empty blue. The stage is set at one end, backed up against the blank wall, which is the west front of the existing cathedral. We can use the door leading into the cloister for stage-left entrances and exits. But we'll need some kind of curtained backdrop for the stage-right exits, and we'll have to tape down the cables so that no one electrocutes themselves creeping round behind the stage. I say, George, did you check that our insurance cover is extended to include Europe? Be just our luck if one of the audience gets sizzled to a crisp.

The acoustic is unsympathetic. It doesn't float upwards too much, but gets lost in the chapels. There is some traffic noise, but the festival management will close off the cathedral precinct. The disturbance should be minimal. You can't ever eliminate fire engines and aeroplanes completely. Our real problem is linguistic. The festival is international. The marketing ideology stresses interpretations of Shakespeare, concentrating on his infamous universal significance. We have therefore, performing just before us, an all-male Japanese *kabuki* *Macbeth* with black and white masks and platform soles, a Romanian circus troupe doing A *Midsummer Night's Dream* with trapezes and clowns and *Coriolanus* danced by Argentinians, with all the steps based on the tango. George watched them rehearse. He says that Aufidius and Coriolanus dancing the tango with daggers in their hands gave him an erection. He is worried that we will look too conventional.

'In Elizabethan costume, darling? Don't let it worry your pretty little head. We have tub-thumping punch-ups and we're wildly camp. To a French audience doublet and hose will seem as outrageous as if we were all dressed as Zulus.'

This is perfectly true. But how do we stop them fidgeting if they can't understand the dialogue? I've got it!

SUBTITLES!

Not every word, of course, but a bit like the silent movies. A general summary of the action on a huge yellow tape which is unravelled at the front of the stage just below the actors. Scroll left to right like a news-flash on the television. Quick! Get Valeria to *parlez-vous Français* with Delphine, our festival liaison officer, and we'll have the whole thing set up by Friday. We can't try ourselves out in the space until then anyway because the Midsummer Night's Dreamers are swinging to and fro in the vault with no net beneath them.

Getting the pitch of our voices right in the muggy air is a bit of a problem. We will begin our performances at nine, just as it's getting dark, and we end well after mid-night. One interval. We are giving three performances. George is biting his nails. The tango has sold out, but we haven't. The nightmares of open-air performances begin. Valeria is chewed up by mosquitoes and her left cheek looks like a gnarly carrot. The subtitles, lit from below, resemble the adverts for Summer Sales at Renault. And now a word from our sponsors. The back rows will need binoculars to see them. Persuading the subtitles to unravel at the same speed as the performance is giving me kittens. Finally I lay my hands on a walkie-talkie link-up. I watch the show from the back and whisper commands into Delphine's petite ears. Once the walkie-talkie is working the whole thing scrolls seamlessly from left to right, its giant letters in immaculate French, checked by a chap from the local Fac, giving the effect of a Gothic televi-sion set of gigantic proportions with the action helpfully explained below. It works! It works! We've got subtitles. And I'm back with Morning Glory, hearing all the gossip and picking up the threads. We've found the best local watering hole for theatricals and Valeria is having a torrid affair with one of the Japanese actors, who, once he'd got his make-up off, is a jolly, giggling chap with a round face and perfect English. She makes him put the mask back on when they're having sex, but she says he spoils the effect by giggling inside the dammed thing and if she hears him laughing she can't come. He teases her for falling in love, not with him, but with a menacing impassive Oriental. James has a go on the Romanian trapeze. George sees him doing it and needs three whiskies to get over the horror, the horror, of almost losing our leading man two nights before lift-off. As always I am very philosophical.

'If he dies, darling, you'll just have to play Lear and I'll take over as Kent.'

'You're on,' George murmurs weakly. The whole thing is like one big hair-raising holiday.

What with the Morning Glory's collective hysterias and creating the subtitles, I haven't seen the neighbours, Mathilde or Nicole, nor been inside the restaurant for over ten days. I pop home to pick up some clean knickers and do all Morning Glory's smalls in the machine. As soon as I've got my key in the lock, Mathilde hurtles out of the neighbours' front door yelling,

'Stylo! Stylo!'

They were a little alarmed by my vanishing act. The boys were convinced that I'd been made away with by the violent actor and given one more day they'd have dredged the reservoir and begun searching the *garrigue* with sticks and dogs. Bernard wanted to make a *déposition* at the Gendarmerie. Maman had begun to look grim and was about to reach a decision. And so I am forced to reassure them and reveal that I am involved in the Shakespeare festival. I know I should have told another story. But the simplicity of the truth is much more plausible. Everybody's heard of sodding Shakespeare. The worst is upon me. They are desperate to see the show and support Stylo, *jusqu'au bout*. But at this stage I fail to grasp the moral of the play. As long as you can say, this is the worst, it's not the worst. The worst is yet to come.

I rationalize, driving back down the long roads to Narbonne, over the Aude and across the marshy flats, all the poplars shining, astir in the warm wind. They've seen George once, in drag, in an old photo. He looks quite different in a grass skirt with coconut falsies. And tomorrow night he'll be decked out to the gunnels in greasepaint and soft velvet hats. OK, so his voice is distinctive, but what have they heard? A lot of muffled Renaissance shouting. Also, and this is my trump card, they think he's gone. They won't expect to see him. You only ever see what you expect to see. That's why married women get away with adultery so easily. Their husbands never think that someone else might fancy the old bag. No, all is well. But I'll make sure that the complimentary tickets aren't in the front row.

Hooray everyone! The first performance has sold out.

We have been advertised as The Royal Shakespeare Company in a classic production etc., etc., with some choice quotes translated from the *Financial Times*. I was right. Radical acting, by Apollo! Doublet and hose, with real swords and no gimmicks. When the lights intensify and George is standing there in velvet hat and embroidered codpiece with Gloucester and Edmund, my heart is pumping, not with fright, but pride. Concentrate hard on the unfolding subtitles, woman, that's your job.

I thought the king had more affected the Duke of Albany than Cornwall.

Go. Go. Go.

The audience is hypnotized. They grasp the fact that it's a family row with no trouble whatsoever. My Lords France and Burgundy are applauded to the patriotic echo. Edmund is excessively sexy in skin-tight green with an enormous sequined device around the privates. Our production could well set the style for the winter collections. The subtitles are mesmerizing. The idea was sheer genius. I am thinking of recycling the technique at English matinées for schools. Shakespeare may as well be written in Latin for all that they can understand.

The first act is a stonking success. The girls are extraordinary. All malice and vindictiveness. Valeria has surpassed herself as Goneril. But I hear the first crackle of thunder, far away, at the moment when Edmund cries out, down the entire length of this bewitching Gothic car park, *'Now Gods, stand up for bastards!'* His obscene gesture, George's idea no doubt, brings the house down.

I start praying.

Thou, Nature, art my goddess. Just hold the storm till Act III. O reason not the need, if you piss down now the show will be ruined. I am transfixed by the subtitles and anxiety at the approaching thunder. This is just too damned realistic. We have taped sound effects; there's no bloody need for verismo. George is doing over Oswald wonderfully well. I've now heard him do this speech dozens of times while I was splicing it into the domestic violence tape. *'A knave, a rascal, an eater of broken meats, a base, proud, shallow, beggarly, three-suited, hundred-pound, filthy, worsted-stocking knave . . .'* No, no George, you've got the emphasis wrong. And the pace. Faster, more like bullets from an automatic. Shakespearian invective needs to sound like Maman bawling out Louise. Faster, with more venom. '. . . *and art nothing but the composition of a knave, beggar, coward, pander, and the son and heir of a mongrel bitch.'* Good, Good, that's better. O Lord, that was fork lightning in the south west!

CRACK! Thick yellow bolts, with an afterflash that remains on the eyeball, and then a gigantic splintering crash like falling timber, which circles in the upper air. The entire audience rustles and looks up, alarmed. The electric charge actually makes the tips of my fingers tingle. George ups the volume and then we are surrounded by huge gusts of thunder, collapsing columns falling in the sky. I look anxiously at the rising mass of unfinished Gothic. The heat suddenly increases in the watery air and the sounds appear to chase each other from place to place. Again and again, a giant luminous glow overcomes the dark. The storm comes closer, draws back, comes closer again. I order Delphine to unravel some more of the subtitles. Quick, quick, before we're all electrocuted and washed away.

In fact the coming storm enhances the performance. We're not that far in, but it's magnificent. Go to it, George!

> *'Sir, 'tis my occupation to be plain:*
> *I have seen better faces in my time*
> *Than stands on any shoulder that I see*
> *Before me at this instant.'*

His glare includes the audience. And then, above the thunder, comes a piercing shriek, eight rows back.

'C'est lui ! c'est lui! That's the man who beat up Stylo!'

Oh no. This is the worst.

Mathilde, loyal to the last, has forgotten herself completely and is on her feet.

'Which one? Where? Where? Get him!'

Laurent, Bernard, Jean-Yves and Maman are still programmed in commando mode. They have overturned their chairs. They are heading for the stage.

'Stop them with the subtitles,' I shriek down the walkie-talkie to Delphine.

The neighbours burst through the subtitles and fling themselves upon George.

The heavens open and with a dull crack all the lights go out. Somebody screams. The amphitheatre is in chaos. I'll never know whether this was a blessing or a catastrophe. As I push my way towards the stage I can hear Albany and Cornwall trying to fend off my neighbours, who, like righteous crusaders, are bent on making a citizen's arrest.

'I say, old chaps, let up a bit.'

Oswald catches Bernard by the heels and trips him up. But the attacker who manages to give George a giant box round the ears is Maman. I can hear it from here. The audience is haring away to the exits, still glowing green in the dark, fending off the deluge with their programmes. God bless the fire officer and his emergency generator. No one has noticed the *mêlée* on stage. I go racing round to the cloister. From the door which was our stage-left entrance, I can see a punch-up in progress that would thrill many a director of Spaghetti Westerns.

'George! George! Run or they'll kill you!'

He still has his hat on as he comes spinning off the stage into the cloister. We hurtle into the Bishop's Palace precinct and out the back door down the main drag. George sprints ahead in his tights, clutching his codpiece. I am about to have a stroke. The blood is exploding in my eyeballs.

Café du Balcon. Quick. Through to the back. It is a local café. No tourists. Only the old men and video game fanatics who inhabit bars like this one all over France. The chairs are wooden and rickety. We fling ourselves down, gasping. My trousers are soggy round the knees. George's make-up is running in streaks down his face. He looks like a tramp in velvet and feathers. The waiter stands beside us, incredulously peering down at George's embroidered codpiece.

'Two beers,' I roar in English, hysterical.

'Calm down, old girl,' says George, 'and tell me what the hell is going on. What in God's name have the audience got against me?'

'They think you've been beating me up,' I sigh wearily.

George stares, open-mouthed.

'All right, Henry,' he snaps, 'come clean. What on earth have you done? What have you told them?'

'Certainly not the truth.'

Four beers later, George is laughing, bent double over the table, his marvellous short cape à la Walter Raleigh vibrating with chuckles. All the occupants of the café are looking at us. We are clearly drunk, mad and English.

'But what can I do now?' I wail wretchedly. The performance has been cancelled. The storm is beginning to ease.

'What can you do, old thing? Plan B. You're going to learn the part of Kent tonight. We'll sit up all night and recite it together if we have to. Nine a.m. rehearsals of all your scenes with the cast. And then back on the boards with you. I can't go on; I'll only get attacked. Did you know there's a men-only nude beach at Narbonne? I've read all about it in my *Pink Guide for Gay Travellers*. And if you need me, then that's where I'll be, improving my tan and getting my eye in. I've had quite enough of *King Lear* anyway. I'm taking a holiday.'

He reaches across the table and gives me a sticky hug, which leaves a smear of greasepaint all down one cheek. And there we sit, our spare tyres wobbling helplessly with laughter.

Everyone who wanted to leave it at Act I got their money back and we did an extra performance on the Sunday. Considering what had actually happened, the front-page coverage was very sedate and only mentioned the weather. But there was a long analysis of the universal significance of the storm as metaphor, which made *King Lear* so intriguing for those who hadn't seen it that all three subsequent performances sold out, twice over. A grisly publicity photo of Cornwall putting out Gloucester's eyes with the spurs on his boots must have helped. And there was a really extraordinary translation of 'OUT, VILE JELLY!' as the headline. Our business manager walked up and down alongside the queue for returns, gloating. Delphine repaired the subtitles and our usual props assistant took over from me with the walkie-talkie. Her French wasn't very good, so there was the odd slippage in the relationship between the subtitles and the action. Nobody noticed. Maman read me an awful lecture about women who go back to violent men. I knew I was in for a scorcher when she opened up with, 'It's none of my business, but . . .' and hung my head in shame.

I was quite a hit in the part of Kent. Mathilde and Maman were among my greatest fans. They attended every performance. I don't think I'll take up acting again, but I like to think that I have made the part of Kent my own. With George's help, of course. But I have given it my emphasis.

AUTHOR'S NOTE

I first conceived *Seven Tales* as a literary response to the B-movies I enjoy watching, late at night, on French television. I sleep badly sometimes and have discovered, to my surprise, that if I watch the horror film at 12.20, the horror remains in the box and not in my head. I then sleep very well. And so I decided to write a sequence of linked tales, which explored first person narratives through different voices and directly engaged with the clichés I was watching, generated largely, but not exclusively, by American film culture. These are the narrative clichés of late night TV in France: rape, terrorism, sexual abuse, perverted desires, the uncanny and the supernatural, poltergeists, vampires and aliens, serial killers, stalkers (also usually serial killers), domestic violence, pornography and mass murder. The victims in all these narratives are usually women.

I wrote tales because this is the medium within which writers in every tradition have always explored subjects that are taboo in the daylight world. These tales are nightpieces. I refused to toe the line of political correctness, middle-class morality and good taste. This was deliberate. I was interested in characters who were amoral, vindictive and unforgiving, but who could argue their case with a rational persuasiveness that carried conviction. They weren't all monsters. Two of my speakers, large, middle-aged and enterprising, wandered through potentially devastating events with an insouciance and humour that I have found well worth imitating.

The tales are deliberately linked to one another. 'Moving' and 'The Strike' are both tales of apocalypse. 'My Emphasis' is a comic version of similar material treated in 'Small Arms'. At some time or another we all want to kill the neighbours, but even I, until I wrote 'My Emphasis', had never imagined that domestic violence could be hilarious. The *Seven Tales* were written to disturb and to provoke. I want my readers to revisit the clichés of sexuality and violence, to read them afresh – and to think again.

ACKNOWLEDGEMENTS

I am grateful to the following people for their help, encouragement and support while I was writing this book: Monsieur and Madame Alexis, Pete Ayrton, Alison Ball, René and Nicole Cottet-Emard, Joan Crawford, Will Datson, Richard Duncker, Miranda and Matilda Duncker, Dave Evans, Victoria Hobbs, Anne Jacobs, Peter Lambert, Jacqueline Martel, Jenny Newman, Menna Phillips, Alexandra Pringle, Madame Mimi Rubio, Myriam Rubio, David Shuttleton, and Nicole Thouvenot. Thank you to Claude Châtelard for her French expertise. Needless to say all the errors are mine. As always, my deepest debt is to S.J.D.

Earlier versions of four of these tales were previously published in the following books and newspapers. I would like to thank the respective editors and publishers for their kind permission to reprint my work.

'Sophia Walters Shaw' in *Ovid Metamorphosed* Ed. Philip Terry (Chatto & Windus, 2000), pp. 78–109.

'Moving' *Express on Sunday Magazine,* 13 June 1999.

'Paris' *The Time Out Book of Paris Short Stories* Ed. Nicholas Royle (Penguin Books, 1999), pp. 1–12.

'Stalker' *New Writing 8* Eds. Tibor Fischer and Lawrence Norfolk (Vintage, 1999), pp. 1–39.

I finished this manuscript while on retreat at Hawthornden Castle in Scotland. Thank you to the Director, Administrator and staff at Hawthornden for the opportunity to work in ideal conditions.